D0108667

KILLER'S RIGHTS

KILLER'S RIGHTS

Nan Hamilton

Walker and Company ✹ New York

For John, who always encourages me
to widen my horizons

Copyright © 1984 by Pat Ball

All rights reserved. No part of this book may
be reproduced or transmitted in any form or by
any means, electric or mechanical, including
photocopying, recording, or by any information
storage and retrieval system, without permission
in writing from the Publisher.

All the characters and events portrayed in this
story are fictitious.

First published in the United States of America
in 1984 by the Walker Publishing Company, Inc.

Published simultaneously in Canada by John Wiley & Sons
Canada, Limited, Rexdale, Ontario.

84196?

Library of Congress Cataloging in Publication Data
Hamilton, Nan.
Killer's rights
I. Title.
PS3558.A4434K5 1984   813'.54   83-14746
ISBN 0-8027-5579-8
Library of Congress Catalog Card Number: 83-14746
Printed in the United States of America
10 9 8 7 6 5 4 3 2

I

Roy Morgan parked his inconspicuous blue car on one of Pacoima's drabber side streets about two blocks from where he was going. He didn't want the car associated with Hokey's Place. As he got out, the late afternoon sun poured heat over him with ninety-five-degree fervor. He stared down the narrow street with its old-style bungalows and dried-up lawns. It reminded him of where he'd grown up—faded square houses filled with dull square people.

He took a pair of sunglasses out of his shirt pocket and put them on. They were part of his California image. More important, he liked the psychological advantage they gave him over other people. It amused him to watch them try to talk a deal to two unrevealing squares of brown glass.

He knew he was early, but he liked it that way—no surprises. On the short walk to Hokey's Place, he passed a small community college in the midst of its four o'clock exodus. He'd never been to college. His higher education, begun in the streets, had been a curriculum of mugging, burglary, armed robbery and various jail terms. The lessons had been readily absorbed and had left no trace on his clean-cut good looks. Early in life he'd found that his appearance was a prime asset, so he took care of it. He'd stayed off the heavy stuff, kept in shape. In Folsom, where he'd done his hard time, he'd worked out regularly, even studied some. It had broken the monotony and eventually, coupled with his earnest boyish appeal, it had conned the parole board into an early release. People tended to trust him; he always made the most of that.

Strolling past the campus on his way to Hokey's, he surveyed the students lounging on the lawn or heading home. One or two recent customers avoided his eyes. Scared, middle-class junkies—he despised them. A pair of coeds stopped talking to size him up in frank appraisal. Tight jeans and a tapered shirt open to reveal the pelt of fine gold hair on his chest gave him the sexy look he cultivated. He could almost hear their little minds ticking over—"Did you see that? God, I bet he's good in bed!" He could have picked them up easily if he'd wanted to, but they were dime-a-dozen stuff. He looked them over lazily and walked on.

Morgan grinned, enjoying it as he always did—eat your heart out baby, it's not your lucky day! Their kind of sex was like food, a pleasurable necessity for a man of his drive. But where it was really at for him— He chopped the thought off abruptly. It was too damned risky even thinking about it.

When he reached Hokey's Place, the run-down burger stand he'd picked for his meeting with Flaco, he ordered a burger, malt and a bag of fries. As he waited for his order, he checked out the only other customers, a couple of kids nursing Cokes at a far table—no problem. When he was served, he took the food over to one of the fly-specked tables on the patio and sat down. After a bite of the sandwich, he pushed it aside. The malt was chalky; one sip was enough. For sure, no cops would choose Hokey's for a Code Seven. He picked up the bag of fries, held it just below the table edge for a moment, then set it down again.

He drummed his fingers irritably as he waited for Flaco to show, trying to ignore the smell of stale grease from the grill. The Mex was still probably trying to scratch up the green. Five more minutes, Morgan decided, then he'd split.

Within three, Flaco showed up—anxiety and apology all over his face. He went up to order a Coke at the window. That was one of Morgan's rules—keep it natural. Then, his thin face strained with an ingratiating smile, he slid onto the bench beside Morgan.

"Yo, man, pretty good place you pick to meet."

"If you can stand the food," Morgan muttered, eyeing his uneaten hamburger with distaste.

"We ain't here for food, man." Flaco dropped his voice to a whisper. "You got it?"

"First let's have the green." Morgan stared at Flaco, the sunglasses giving him the look of an idol with brown glass eyes.

"Yeah, sure, right here." Unnerved, Flaco fumbled in his pants pocket a moment. Then, taking a fresh couple of napkins out of the table holder, he handed them to Morgan. They covered five bills nicely.

Morgan wiped his mouth on the napkins, then dropped his hands to his lap. "Have some fries," he said as he pocketed the bills.

Flaco stiffened, red with anger. Morgan smiled contemptuously and pushed the bag toward him. When Flaco picked it up he felt the small lumps in the bottom. Opening the bag, he took out a limp fry and ate it as he counted the small balloons just visible beneath the rest of the soggy potatoes. Then he stuffed the bag into his pocket and turned eagerly to Morgan.

"Hey, man, I could do you some good—" he began, then stopped. Roy Morgan wasn't listening; he was watching a girl who'd come out of the small grocery store down the street. As she walked toward them, he automatically eyed the body outlined by her thin summer dress. She had no breasts to speak of, a waist so small she looked like she'd break if you touched her, but nice long legs.

Flaco, now that he was set again, took time to enjoy her too. He leaned back in macho nonchalance and made a small "O" with his fingers.

[3]

The girl felt them staring and slowed her pace, staring back. There was no self-conscious invitation in her almond-shaped eyes, only curiosity and, to Morgan's annoyance, amusement.

Not sure why he did it, Morgan took off his sunglasses and smiled at her. She smiled back—an innocent child's smile, sunny and clean. Then, unexpectedly, she rounded her fingers against her eyes to imitate glasses and solemnly surveyed him, her head cocked to one side like a speculative robin. Then she dropped her hands, as if tired of the game, nodded to Flaco and went on her way.

Morgan turned around in his seat to look after her, watching the long black ponytail of her hair twitching slightly just above that fragile hand-span waist. He could almost feel it between his hands.

"Who is she?" he asked, his voice not quite steady. Unconsciously his fingers toyed with the gold chain he wore, smoothing the two small charms at the bottom—a tiny bicycle and a miniature violin.

The expression on Morgan's face bothered Flaco. "Hey, man," he said, "cool it. Don't waste your time on that one. Her old she-dragon mother watches her like the crown jewels or somethin'." Nervously he bit at a fingernail as he eyed the kiddy charms on Morgan's chain. Pretty kinky things for a macho guy to wear. Word was out that Morgan had done hard time and had big connections with the Brotherhood. What the hell! He was selling what Flaco had to buy.

Putting on his glasses again, Morgan turned the brown squares on Flaco. "I said, what's her name?"

"Yumi Kubota. Her old lady runs the mom-and-pop store down the street, but there ain't no Pop, just the old lady and Yumi."

The way Morgan was smiling made Flaco think he'd better wise him up about Yumi. "Hey, man, you're new around here, so maybe you don' know—the guys lay off Yumi. We don' let no guy bother her she don' want."

Morgan said nothing, but his mouth hardened.

Flaco hated trying to see through those goddamned sunglasses. "Sure she looks like any chick, but inside, man, she's just a little kid. She's a dummy, too, can't hear or speak."

Morgan examined his well-polished fingernails. "Forget I asked. She's a Jap anyway."

Flaco let his breath out in relief, but the slur burned. He knew Morgan's contempt was for him, too, but he didn't dare show his feelings. He needed the bastard.

"Get lost, bud." Morgan didn't even look at him.

Flaco mouthed a silent obscenity and, allowing himself a small defiance, took out a broken pocket comb and ran it through his hair, taking his time. Only then did he stand up and walk away. When he was out on the sidewalk, he spat into the street and looked back. The son of a bitch was still sitting there playing with his fancy chain, and smiling.

Morgan rubbed his fingers gently across the small bicycle charm. It was a souvenir from the first one—no shoes or ribbons in the closet for him. It was a kicky thing getting the bike charm because that's how he'd worked it—offering to fix the flat tire on her bike. She'd followed him like a puppy to where he'd said his tools were, hero-worshipping him with her kid's smile. He could still see her—big blue eyes, soap and water shine on her face, a spiky blond pigtail, her young body just beginning to promise curves. Then, when he'd pulled her down behind the bushes—man, how she'd kicked and thrashed, her head twisting from side to side. If she hadn't started screaming so loud maybe he wouldn't have choked her. His fingers curled now, clutching the edge of the wooden table as if they retained a memory of their own—the feel of the delicate bones of her throat. That had been the best part of all. Almost unconsciously Morgan picked up the chalky malt and sipped to relieve the dryness of his mouth.

The violin kid hadn't been nearly as good as he thought she'd be when he followed her across the vacant lot in the rain. She'd tried to beat him off with the damn violin. One good punch had stopped that. But then she'd lain there like a rag doll, sobbing and hiccupping, too scared to fight. It was only when he'd reached for her throat that the exhilaration had swept over him as before, heightened by the light drizzle of rain and the smell of the wet grass.

Morgan's palms grew sweaty and he balled his fists against his thighs. He'd gotten away with it twice. He'd get away with it this time. And this one would be really something. Too bad he'd asked Flaco the girl's name. That was careless. But there were ways to take care of Flaco if necessary. Smiling, Morgan slipped the gold chain inside his shirt and buttoned the lower buttons. He'd be at Hokey's again tomorrow. He had to find out for himself where Yumi lived.

II

ABOUT the same time the next afternoon, Morgan was nursing a Coke at Hokey's when the girl came out of the grocery store. He kept his back turned until she had passed, then crossed to the other side of the street and followed her. Her bright yellow dress made her easy to watch, even from the careful half-block he kept between them. He saw her turn into the fenced yard of a small white frame house, waited until she'd gone inside, then walked toward it. It was a corner house framed by an overgrown hedge of pink oleanders. He didn't slow his steps but turned the corner and continued past the yard until the street ended in a narrow alley. A wooden fence with a gate enclosed the property on that side.

He had been thinking about the girl since the day before, with a shuddering longing of anticipation. The idea of her alone in the house was tempting. He hesitated at the alley, but alarm bells were ringing in his head. He had a contact to make in a few hours that he didn't dare mess up. Besides, there were too many unknown factors to make it safe—the old lady for one.

He walked on around the block, then back past Hokey's to the Kubota Grocery Store. It was empty when he entered except for a chunky-looking Japanese woman he guessed must be Yumi's mother. Her graying hair was long and piled on top of her head with a pair of black lacquer pins stuck through the knot.

"Yes?" The woman looked at him, waiting.

He said quickly, "Got any beer?"

"Beer over there." She pointed to the cooler in the back of the store. He went to it, picked out a six-pack, then took his time looking over the selection of cheeses, wondering how best to get the information he wanted. He watched the woman slit open the top of a carton of canned goods with a knife, then bend over to lift it up to the counter. That was the opening he needed.

He hurried over to her. "Here, let me help you. That's heavy!"

Surprised, Mrs. Kubota looked up at her customer's boyish, smiling face. He set his beer down and lifted the carton easily onto the counter. "*Arigato*—thank you!" She bowed slightly, letting the tired lines of her face relax into a smile.

"Don't you have any help?" Morgan's tone was sympathetic.

"I no need. All OK. Daughter help sometime. Boy help sometime."

Morgan took out money for the beer, then noticed a Japanese doll in a glass case standing beside the register. It was a young girl doll in a bright red kimono, gracefully holding a ball as if about to throw. The painted face with its wide innocent eyes and soft pink mouth was remarkable. A flow of black hair with a fringe that brushed the forehead looked just like silk. He wanted to touch it. It was Yumi in the glass case waiting for him. He didn't realize he'd been staring until the woman said, "You like doll? My daughter make."

"Is it for sale?" Morgan asked. The shuddering was starting inside him again.

"Yes. For sale, twenty dollar. Is real hair. Case extra, ten dollar. You want to buy?"

"Just the doll." Without moving his eyes from the doll, he fished for his wallet.

"You have little girl?" Mrs. Kubota asked as she took the money.

"No." Morgan hesitated. "It's a present."

[8]

The answer seemed to satisfy the woman. She reached for paper to gift-wrap the doll.

Impatiently he watched her make up the package. Then he realized he'd almost forgotten to get the information he needed. As he picked up his beer and took the neatly wrapped package he said, "I'm new to the neighborhood. How late are you open?"

"Every night nine o'clock. Close Sunday." Mrs. Kubota folded her pudgy hands across her waist and said proudly, "Have best fruit, vegetable, even little meat."

"Well, great!" Morgan moved toward the door. "I like a small store like this; I'll be seeing you."

He walked back toward his car, trying to keep his eyes off the package cradled in his arm. So Yumi's mother stayed at the store until nine every night except Sunday. There was no Pop. He could pick his time—"but never on Sunday." He laughed to himself at the small joke, then sobered. But not tonight either. He had business. Yumi would have to wait. He unlocked the car and got in.

He tore the paper wrapping off the doll and sat caressing the silky hair. The old lady had said it was real hair. Was it Yumi's? Sweat beaded his upper lip and he licked it off with his tongue. The doll's innocent eyes stared up at him. His hand tightened around the tiny body as his insides churned. Holding the doll was like a preview of the real thing. Reluctantly he placed her on the seat beside him, close to his thigh, and started the engine.

At ten that night Morgan was at St. Jude's Summer Carnival waiting beside the Ferris wheel for his contact, whom he didn't know by sight. To pass the time, he drank a can of beer and studied the crowd. A balding man with the arms of a prizefighter came and stood next to him, watching the wheel go round as he munched on a hot dog. When he had finished eating he looked over at Morgan. "Message from Danny."

Morgan turned his head fractionally and stared at the man. "Not sure I know any Danny."

"You know him—from the joint." Almost casually the big man began to scratch his arm, pushing up the sleeve of a gaudy red and yellow Hawaiian shirt. His dirty fingernails dug across the reddening flesh.

Among the welter of tattoos that covered the beefy arm, Morgan saw the one that counted—three intertwined sixes. "I remember Danny now. If you're in touch with him, tell him Morgan sends regards."

The connection was made; the man nodded. "I'm Mike. Heard a lot about you, Morgan. Let's talk."

He walked over to the operator of the Ferris wheel and flicked a quick thumbs-up sign. Almost at once the big wheel slowed and stopped. When they were aboard, it started again. They were swung up and out over the lighted booths and the milling crowd.

Neither man noticed the Chicano staring at their swaying perch with curious eyes. Flaco itched to know what was up. He didn't know the big guy with Morgan, but information about the meeting might be worth a balloon or two in the right quarters. He decided to hang around and see what happened.

When they reached the top of the wheel, Mike came to the point.

"Danny wants a job done, Morgan. One of your specialties."

There was only one answer to that. Danny was top dog in the Brotherhood. What he asked for, he got. "OK," Morgan said, "give me the dope."

Shrieks from the spiraling Loop-the-Loop nearby scratched across the night. Morgan stared at the crazily revolving bullet cabins, feeling as trapped as the suckers inside them. He didn't want any extra heat now when things were going so well.

He'd joined the Brotherhood in Folsom. It was necessary to belong to one of the major prison gangs to survive. They had protected him as promised, but they always collected for their services. Morgan's debt was bigger than most. Like a good executive, Danny had recognized his special qualities. So they'd set him up with the necessary connections outside. Now he was making it big as a dealer, but, as he'd learned the hard way, nothing came for free.

"It's Smokey Trotter," Mike was saying. "Know him?"

"Local supplier, Black Guerrilla Family. I know him."

Morgan was interested now. Smokey was the local competition. He could be doing himself a favor, too.

"Danny wants him wasted. He said to do it your way, Morgan, no hardware."

Why Smokey had to be wasted Morgan neither knew nor cared. "His" way, Danny had said. Unconsciously he gripped the wooden bar that pinned him to the seat and stared down at his hands dispassionately. They were as lethal as years of street fighting and professional karate training could make them. He'd developed his own style, a mix of karate and Kung Fu. It made him superior to most. That was "his" way— he needed no other weapons. The wheel was swinging down toward the lights in a fast arc. The air whipped against his face, triggering in his body the old excitement of a kill.

"Make a clean job of it, Morgan, and watch your back." Mike's gravelly voice broke into his thoughts. "Smokey's a big honcho. The Guerrillas and the Nuestra Familia will be after the guy that wastes him, or any other brother they can find. That puts you right on the shit list."

"I can handle it." Morgan toughed it out, though he knew the danger was real. His first day in prison, his cellmate, a

[11]

soldier of the Black Guerrilla Family, one of the most power-ful prison gangs, had been found in the laundry stabbed in the head with a shank. Before an official investigation was even in gear, a guy from the Mexican Mafia was strangled in the exercise yard. It turned out he hadn't made the hit, but the debt was paid. That was why Morgan had joined the Brotherhood.

More than once in prison, he'd heard orders given to waste an enemy soldier on the outside, even though one of the Brotherhood or their allies, Mexican Mafia, would be sacri-ficed in return. You could leave prison, but never the gang. Your orders came from men like Danny, and you obeyed or you were a dead man. His stomach tightened with each jerk-ing stop as the big wheel made its way to the ground. Smokey was big profit to the Black Guerrilla Family. Taking him out could start a full-scale war. Maybe he'd have to get away for a while. Damn it! Things were going just right and now there was Yumi. Maybe there'd still be time for her before it heated up. He realized Mike had been saying something and caught the end of it. "They won't know who hit him," Morgan prom-ised. "Tell Danny I'll take care of it."

Mike nodded, satisfied. "OK, let's get off this thing." He signaled to the operator.

When they got off the wheel Morgan hung back, lighting a cigarette, until Mike disappeared into the crowd. Then he began to walk in the opposite direction, past the booths toward the exit. His mind was on the Smokey job. He didn't notice Flaco fall in behind him. It gave him a grim sort of amusement to realize that this time he'd have to disguise his handiwork. He was totally unprepared when the crowd thinned momentarily and a flash of yellow caught his eye. It was Yumi.

She was standing in front of the pitch ball booth clinging to the arm of a thin Japanese. Morgan sized him up and dismissed him as no problem. Yumi seemed all excited. She pointed toward the booth, let go of the man's arm to move her hands gracefully in quick darting gestures. Then she pulled him toward the counter and pointed again, this time to the row of pink teddy bears that were the prizes. Amused, Morgan watched the guy give in. He bought six balls, then wound up to throw. The first one missed, the next hit, the third missed. Yumi looked disappointed. The second set was again one out of three.

Morgan moved up beside them, letting his shoulder brush against Yumi's. She glanced up at him and edged away a little. Morgan bought six balls while she tried to coax her friend into another try. He was shaking his head no when Morgan began to throw.

He fired the six balls in rapid succession—six balls, six hits. There was a small round of applause from the crowd. With a modest smile he looked down at Yumi, who was clapping with the rest.

"Here's your prize, mister." The girl running the booth handed over one of the teddy bears. Morgan took it, appeared slightly embarrassed, and then, as if on inspiration, turned to Yumi. "Would you like to have it?" He held it out to her.

Her face lit with pleasure as she took it from him with the eagerness of a child. She gave him a shy smile, then nuzzled the furry head against her shoulder.

"Say, that's nice of you!" her companion said, smiling. "How about having a beer with us? My name's Ken Kimura."

Morgan brought his attention back from Yumi. "Thanks, but no. I've got a date."

Yumi looked up at him and smiled; she needed no words. It was obvious that she thought he was Prince Charming in person. She'd welcome him with open arms when he came calling. Morgan smiled down at her, then he turned his back and made for the exit. He walked unseeing down the crowded midway, his mind filled with fantasy pictures of Yumi. His fingers found the gold chain and caressed the two small charms. He'd be adding a new one soon, and he knew what it would be—a small gold teddy bear.

His mind was still busy with plans for Yumi when he reached his car. He never noticed the battered motorbike that trailed him all the way to his apartment.

III

A FEW days later, while lounging at ease in the air-conditioned comfort of his apartment, Morgan read the few lines in the newspaper about the death of Smokey Trotter—"savagely beaten by unknown assailants." He smiled in satisfaction. His plan and his caution had paid off. He'd managed to ambush Smokey, "high" and incautious, as he'd left his girlfriend's apartment in the middle of the night. One quick, silent chop had finished the bastard. Best of all, local rumor had it that her former boyfriend had put out the contract on Smokey.

He stretched the fingers of his right hand, admiring their iron hardness. The tricky part, distasteful, but vital to his plan, had been carrying Smokey's lifeless body to a vacant lot half a block down the deserted street. There he'd administered the "savage beating" to suggest more than one attacker.

Now he could plan his visit to Yumi. He hadn't as yet ordered the charm, but this would be the day—for everything. Smiling, he closed his eyes and thought about Yumi. Then he stood up and shook himself. If it was like this now, what would it be with the real thing? He poured himself a stiff drink. Then, stripping off his clothes, he got under a cold, stinging shower until his blood raced. He wanted no cobwebs in his brain when he stalked this one. It must be as good, and as safe, as the other two.

He glanced at his watch. There was still plenty of time to stop at a jeweler's and order the teddy bear charm. He liked things complete to the last detail.

As he had each day since he'd bought it, he picked up the

little Japanese doll and stroked the shiny black hair for a moment. Then, in one quick movement of his strong fingers, he snapped the head from the body. Smiling, he dropped the pieces into the wastebasket.

He looked up the nearest jeweler in the phone book and went there. His business took only a few minutes, after which he drove to Hokey's and parked in the rear where he could watch the sidewalk. When Yumi came out of the grocery, he waited a few minutes before he drove to the house and around the corner, passed it, then pulled into the parking lot of the public library. He took time to think out his approach. The front door was out; somebody might see him there. It would have to be the back door, or a side window. He got out of the car, walked a short distance and turned down the alley. When he came to the Kubotas' back gate and looked into the yard, he knew his luck was in. Yumi was there, kneeling by a small fishpond, her back toward him.

She'd changed her dress for a white flower-printed kimono. He hadn't expected that, but despite the fact that it covered her up from neck to toe, the way it clung to her hips and legs really turned him on. Her tiny waist was spanned by a pink sash. She'd loosened her ponytail so that hair cascaded down her back. A spray of pink oleander was pinned just above her ear with a graceful silver ornament. As she dropped food to the fish she pulled her kimono sleeve back, baring her smooth round arm almost to the shoulder.

Morgan had trouble with his breathing—this was something different—the little doll come to life. He glanced quickly around, checking that the alley was empty and that the heavy oleander hedge screened the side. Then he reached over and flipped the latch on the gate. His nerves jumped at its metallic snap. He expected her to turn around in alarm, but she continued placidly to drop bits of food to the fish. Then he remembered she couldn't hear.

He walked up behind her and lightly touched her shoulder.

She looked up startled. Then she smiled and jumped up, putting both her hands on her knees as she bowed a greeting. Her hair swung forward against her cheek. Morgan could see the soft nape of her neck. He put his hands behind him and kept his smile in place.

Yumi turned and pointed to an old-fashioned glider swing under a tree. Propped against the cushions was the pink teddy bear. She ran over, picked it up, hugged it, then set it down gently and came back to him, still smiling.

Morgan started to speak but she put her fingers against his lips, then against her own, and shook her head. He stood awkwardly, not sure of his next move. His usual line was useless. But Yumi made a drinking gesture and pointed to him. He understood that and nodded. She slipped her small soft hand in his and led him over to the glider, motioning him to sit down. Then she turned and ran into the house.

He was tempted to follow her, but unexpectedly he felt unsure of himself. He even thought about getting up and walking out of the gate. Then he became aware of the lumpy body of the pink teddy bear against his thigh. Almost unconsciously he reached out and smoothed its furry softness. Why should he be nervous? She couldn't even scream.

When Yumi came back with the lemonade for him, Morgan's hand closed gently around hers as he took the glass. He didn't want to frighten her yet. Smiling, she sat down beside him on the glider. As he sipped the drink he felt her studying his face. It bothered him; he finished the lemonade quickly and handed back the glass. Immediately she raised her eyebrows in a question, pointing at the glass. When he shook his head, she set it on the ground. The flower fragrance of her hair excited him. He gestured to her face, her body, then rounded his fingers in the sign of approval. She understood at once and clapped her hands delightedly. Damned if they weren't having a conversation.

He moved closer and the gold chain swung loose from the

deep vee of his white silk shirt. When she saw it, her mouth rounded in a soundless "oh" of pleasure. With a quick, bird-like gesture she picked it up and held it in her hand. The touch of her fingers as they brushed his chest started small chills up and down his body. It was all he could do to restrain himself as she examined each of the gold charms, smiling like a child. Closing her fingers around them she looked at him, brush-stroke eyebrows asking a question. She pointed to herself.

It was plain she was asking for them, but Morgan shook his head no. Still she held the little charms, her soft lips pouting in disappointment as he took them from her, tucking the chain inside his shirt.

She surprised him then by leaning forward and running her fingers over his face, outlining the bone structure. His throat tightened at the light butterfly touch and he eyed her lips, curving and tender and close. He leaned over to kiss her, but quickly she stood up. Angry, Morgan stared at her— the little bitch! Then he saw she wasn't playing games; she was holding out her hand. He took it and allowed her to lead him over to a small garage building he'd barely noticed. God, she was actually asking for it! He followed her inside.

It was a jolt when she turned on the lights and proudly gestured to rows of shelves filled with Japanese dolls in cases, and a long worktable in the center of the floor. It held an unfinished doll and an array of needles, scissors and brushes. She picked up the doll and showed it to him. It was not a Japanese doll; it was a male doll dressed in blue jeans and white silk shirt. It even had a gold chain around its neck and tiny brown glass sunglasses. All it needed was hair. She'd made a freaky doll of him! Damn her.

Smiling, Yumi picked up the doll and pointed to him. Reaching up she touched his hair, then took up a scissors

[18]

and made a cutting motion with it. Morgan jerked and moved away, but like a naughty child she followed him, the scissors poised.

His face contorted with rage, Morgan whipped out his arm and struck her so hard she dropped the doll, fell against the table and slipped to the floor. Her kimono gaped open. As he stared at her, her eyes filled with a silent frantic plea. She tried to pull the kimono closed.

Seeing her that way, helpless and frightened, released all his pent-up violence. He bent over her, his hand twisting in her hair. His foot kicked against the doll and as Yumi stared in terror, he crushed the small body under his heel. Then he pulled her face close to his. She tried to beat at him with her hands, feeble blows that made him want to laugh. He kissed her savagely, his teeth grating against hers.

As her body jerked in her efforts to escape, Morgan laughed, finding this wordless struggle more exhilarating than he'd dreamed. With one hand he gripped her throat, letting her feel the pressure. With the other he ripped away the top of her kimono, exposing her breasts. The pitiful mewing sounds she made inflamed him; he grinned down at her, tightening the pressure on her throat. Then suddenly she stopped struggling. Her head fell back and her eyes closed. Feeling cheated, he shook her savagely and shouted, "Not yet, you little bitch, not yet..."

Suddenly, even in his paroxysm of frustrated rage, he felt blows raining on his head and back. Someone was pulling at him, shouting, "Let her go, you bastard, let her go!"

The flame of his excitement cooled instantly. In one quick motion Morgan turned his body and jumped to his feet. His attacker was the young Japanese who'd been with Yumi at the carnival. His face flushed with anger, he stood ready to fight. But despite his brave karate stance, the nervous flicker of his eyes behind his glasses told Morgan he was scared as hell. He flashed a feeble kick but, grinning, Morgan blocked it.

"You need a few more lessons, Jap." Morgan's fingers, rigid as a sword, thrust into the soft flesh of the boy's diaphragm, making him gasp and fall back. A kick to the jaw threw him backward into the rows of cases, crashing them down with him. Moaning in agony, the boy tried to crawl away. Morgan watched in amusement. "The lesson's not over yet," he grated.

With deliberate slowness he stalked his victim, who crawled painfully around the table, past the open door. Morgan was so intent on his kill that he didn't hear the slight sound behind him. The boy, stumbling to his feet, clutched at his broken glasses with one hand and raised his arm to try to block the fatal blow he knew was coming. Deliberately Morgan aimed a roundhouse kick just under the ribs, toppling him, unconscious. The next quick chop to the throat would kill him. Laughing, Morgan knelt beside the body, its lolling head flung back to expose the boy's thin throat. Morgan formed his fingers into a lethal blade and raised his hand.

He felt his hair seized from behind with a savage tug that made his neck crack as it jerked backward. In sudden shock he stared into the face above him, and focused in horror on the needle-sharp blade aimed at his throat. With an effort he gathered his strength to pull away, but a sudden, sharp agony pierced beneath his collarbone, draining him. His fingers clawed at the spreading, burning pain and recoiled from a sticky wetness. The grip on his hair loosened, and he slumped forward, staring stupidly at the red ooze that stained his hand. His body began to topple slowly to the side, and there was nothing he could do to stop it.

IV

THE stranger glanced into the office of Robbery-Homicide and found it was empty, so he looked around for the nearest source of information. The door marked Juvenile Division was open. He went in there.

"Is Sam O'Hara around? The desk sergeant said he'd be up here, but he's not in his office."

The deep, rich voice carried easily to the office next door, where Sam Ohara sat with Jim Reilly discussing the Smokey Trotter killing. He sighed and leaned back in his chair. "Reagan's got another live one."

Reilly chuckled. "Better go into your act."

They could hear someone helpfully directing the inquirer to the Narcotics Division. "I think he went into Mr. Reilly's office."

Ohara kept his back turned, waiting for Desk Sergeant Reagan's newest pigeon to find him. Firm footsteps advanced, then paused. "I'm looking for Sam O'Hara."

Sam stood up and turned around, his face a careful blank. "I'm Ohara."

Score one for Sergeant Reagan. Despite an effort to control his reaction, the stranger's expression was almost comic. "You're O'Hara?" Disbelief and a suspicion of "wild goose" flashed in his eyes.

"That's right." Ohara had learned to wait it out while the victim registered that Reagan's Irish O'Hara was unmistakably Japanese. "Actually, it's Isamu Ohara, no apostrophe. The Irish is the sergeant's idea." He smiled and held out his hand.

The newcomer shook hands, taking stock of Ohara's six

[21]

feet of well-distributed muscle, long ascetic face and steady black eyes, which seemed to be reading his mind.

Ohara introduced Jim Reilly from Narcotics.

"I'm Ted Washington," the visitor said. "I'll be taking Jake Wozinski's place."

Though Ohara said nothing as he studied the powerful-looking black who stood in front of him, his eyes seemed to frost over. Washington's aggressive stance and the uncompromising look behind the measured smile on his face annoyed him.

"I don't think so." Ohara's voice was cold. "Jake's been my partner for a long time. He'll be out of the hospital soon and back to work."

Washington shrugged. "Personnel assigned me here; sorry if you don't approve." The words were inoffensive, but all the things he kept himself from saying showed in his face. "They call it equal opportunity on-the-job training."

"And that's what you'll get," Ohara said evenly, "but you won't be taking Jake's place."

Ohara recalled last week's memo informing him that a new detective was being assigned to him for orientation. He cooled a little. Perhaps he could understand Washington's slightly pushy attitude better than most; he'd had it himself during his first weeks in Detectives. He'd been only too aware of being a minority pebble in the pool, feeling that, whatever the law said, you had to push a little harder or be overlooked. It had taken awhile to realize that this was one place where it wasn't his origins but how he could hack the job that mattered.

When Sergeant Reagan had first made him a standard joke, his anger had smoldered. Gradually he'd come to understand that it was actually a form of camaraderie. It had made him a member of the club in a way that appealed to his Japanese instincts for subtlety. Remembering, he smiled with more than mere politeness. He could see a little of the tension leave the proud black face.

"All right, Washington, training starts now. Jim and I've been discussing the narcotics connection in the recent Smokey Trotter killing. Are you up on it?"

"What I read in the papers. I think it's a gang killing." Washington apparently didn't believe rookies were to be seen and not heard. "Smokey's probably Black Guerrilla Family."

Reilly looked at Ohara, suppressing a smile. "He probably is," Ohara said and stopped, leaving Washington with the ball he'd grabbed.

Unabashed, Washington ran with it. "I've just come off an organized crime assignment. They needed a new black face for an undercover job in Whittier, so they took me off patrol here and sent me in. I ran into Smokey Trotter there, though it wasn't his territory. I think that's what got him killed; he planned to take it over. When the assignment was finished, I applied for Detectives and got it."

Ohara and Reilly knew that meant Washington had been good at his undercover job. But it took more than that to make a detective.

Washington studied his new training officer's good-looking face but saw no sign that he'd made an impression. All Ohara said was, "Your experience might help. Reilly's checking his files for leads. Suppose you start with him and see what you can come up with. If it's gang related, there could be more than one killing. We'd like to stop that."

"OK," Washington said without expression, but he got the picture; checking the files was as good a way as any of getting him out of the way.

Ohara started for the door. "I've got some paperwork for a court appearance tomorrow. See you later."

He was well aware of what Washington was thinking and feeling just then. Checking the files would seem like busy-work, but it was part of the dull routine that made up the detective's job. It got results. As he walked the short distance to his office across the hall, he realized that Washington was no happier to have him for a training partner than he was to have Washington assigned in Jake's place. Being new was bad enough without being caught up in the old black-Japanese antipathy. Many of the older Japanese felt about blacks the way a lot of whites felt about Orientals. In Japan, the unfortunate children fathered by black soldiers during the occupation were still outcasts in normal society, with no future, no hope. Even in America some of the Issei held on to their prejudice. It was hogwash as far as Ohara was concerned. He'd have to make Washington understand that. It was simply that nobody could really take Jake's place.

He had gotten a solid ten minutes' work in on the court case when the phone rang. He listened, then asked, "Address?"

He wrote rapidly. "I'm on my way."

He was halfway out of the office when he remembered his new responsibility. He sighed and went back to Reilly's office and put his head inside the door. "Washington, drop that for now. We've got a homicide."

Surprise held Washington still for a second before he grabbed his coat from the back of the chair. "Coming!"

When they reached the crime scene, patrol cars had already cordoned off the area. As Ohara parked, Washington saw a flashbulb go off: the police photographer shooting the scene. "They don't waste much time, do they?" he commented.

"All the better for us," Ohara answered as they got out and walked toward the bustle of activity.

The patrol sergeant came up to report. As Ohara listened, his eyes surveyed the immediate area, noting the neighborhood's generally seedy, unprideful appearance: dry stubble yards, scraggly overgrown oleander bushes, paint-thirsty frame houses, almost no traffic. The usual crowd of curious pressed outside the police lines, hoping for a sight of the corpse.

The sergeant called over the young officer who'd answered the call. He looked tense, a bit white about the mouth. Ohara guessed it might be his first homicide. He reported quickly in the police jargon. "Male Cauc., late twenties, stabbed, no witness yet, no ID."

"Who found the body?"

"He did." The officer smiled tentatively as he pointed to a Heinz-57-variety mutt tied to the door of the police car. "We got a barking dog report and came around to handle it."

"Did he mess up the body?"

"No. He was just standing there barking at the bushes. I checked."

"Not much of a witness, is he?" Washington grinned.

"Well, at least he called the police." The young officer's smile broadened, his obvious tension drained away.

Ohara smiled too, knowing that the small joke was just a form of the gallows humor that homicide detectives often found useful for covering a multitude of horrors. The corpse didn't mind. "Let's go see what we've got," he said, and led the way over to the body.

It was lying on its back just under some white oleander bushes. A few petals had drifted over the corpse like frail apologies for the ugliness of death. The body was that of a young, athletic-looking man, dressed in expensive jeans and a white silk shirt. The thick mat of dried crabgrass on which he lay showed no visible marks. "Well, what do you think?" Ohara asked.

Washington, not sure of his role at that point, hadn't expected the question. He'd assumed he was intended to observe in respectful silence. But he fielded it. "Two things, off

[25]

the bat. He doesn't live around here. Those expensive threads don't go with the local population. Wasn't killed here, either. There's not even a stem of those bushes bent, and he's too big to go down without a struggle."

Mentally Ohara gave him good marks for both points as he bent down for a closer look at the body.

"Good-looking dude, wasn't he?" Washington had knelt, too, and was studying the tanned boyish face under its halo of blond curls.

Ohara was thinking the same thing. Thinking also what a waste of a well-developed young body that had so much going for it. They could see the stab wound, just above the collarbone. It was surprisingly small to spill out a life, but there was enough blood to smear the pristine whiteness of the silk shirt and straggle in a dirty rivulet down the man's bronzed chest.

"Stab wound tell you anything?" Ohara asked without looking up.

Washington thought a moment. "When I was working undercover I saw another guy stabbed just like that, same place. I've heard it's a Mafia trademark—almost instantaneous."

"Look at this." Ohara lifted one of the hands. The palm, though not deformed in any way, had a hard edge he recognized. The other hand was the same. "Karate man," he murmured.

Washington had missed that, and it annoyed him. He pointed to the bloodstained fingers. "He lived long enough to know what happened to him."

A darker spot showing beneath the white shirt drew Ohara's eye. Delicately he lifted the clinging silk. Caught in the gold chest hair was another flower petal, pale pink in color. His eyes went to the oleanders fanning above the body. Reaching into his pocket for a glassine envelope, he removed the petal and dropped it in.

Washington reached to retrieve the other fragile white blossoms scattered across the body.

"No, just this pink one," Ohara said. "It probably came from where he was killed." He slipped the envelope into his pocket and stood up, but made no move to go. Staring down at the body, he absorbed the scene through his senses to flesh out the visual image of the lab photos. Even when car doors slammed across the street, he didn't turn his head.

Washington watched the ambulance men unload a stretcher and follow a heavyset man over to the body. Surprised, he heard the man say, "OK, Charlie Chan, what've we got—a sinister new weapon?"

Ohara turned to him, smiling. "Hello, Bob. I hoped it would be you. You'll get a chance to earn your salary on this one."

"With you I always earn it." The man's voice was filled with gloomy resignation. The pathetic expression on his long, pouchy-eyed face made him look like a hungry beagle. Washington fought to keep his own face straight as Ohara introduced them. "This is Bob Abrams, one of our better MEs. Bob, Ted Washington."

Abrams extended his hand. "Hi!" He was not a man to waste words.

Ted Washington returned his greeting, all too conscious that Ohara had not introduced him as his partner.

The deputy ME bent to examine the body, humming an unrecognizable tune as he worked. It made him seem like a happy ghoul, but Washington supposed that when death was an everyday business, you had to keep it impersonal any way you could.

After a few minutes, Abrams looked up and signaled to his ambulance crew that they could take the corpse.

[27]

"Well?" Ohara asked.

"You've got a hole in an unusual place. Whoever did that was an expert."

"Any guess as to when he was killed?" Washington included himself in the conversation.

Abrams turned his big sorrowful eyes on him. "A guess you want? Maybe about twelve hours ago."

"How about the weapon?"

"Oh, ice pick, something like that. I'll be able to tell more when I get inside." He looked down with professional interest at the body being encased in its black rubber sack. "Could be a change of pace, this one."

"Good!" Ohara smiled. "You'll get at it sooner."

"Always sooner he wants," Abrams grumbled. "Tomorrow's the soonest you'll get, Charlie Chan."

Ohara punched him lightly on the shoulder. "I'll settle for that. And by the way, try to get it right, Bob. Charlie Chan isn't Japanese. Try Mr. Moto."

V

Leaving Abrams to supervise the removal of the body, Washington followed Ohara back toward the street. "What now?" he asked.

"Now we start walking and knocking. Which side of the street do you want?"

"I'll take the right; it's shadier." Washington said it with a straight face, but his eyes were amused.

In spite of himself, Ohara was beginning to like this man. "OK. Try to find any kind of witness."

As Ohara started across the street, Washington touched his arm. "Give me a minute." Then he went over to the patrol car where the dog was tied. He bent down and scratched its long shaggy ears, speaking to the officer standing nearby. The dog's tail wagged joyously. Giving him a final pat, Washington went back to Ohara. "Wonder what will happen to the mutt? No ID. They're going to take him to the shelter. "

Ohara looked at the forlorn pooch and shook his head. "That's all they can do. We'd better get cracking."

Separately they covered the entire street and the houses around the corner. When they had finished, they compared notes. They'd turned up only one lead, an old lady in the house opposite the scene. She'd called about the dog and now took the opportunity to complain to Ohara about kids parking their cars on the street at all hours of the night. "Smoking pot, and God knows what else," was how she put it.

"I finally got her down to specifics," Ohara said. "It was one car—old, with a big backseat. She doesn't know when it parked there, but when she got up at one A.M. to get a cup of tea, there it was. She couldn't see anything 'going on,' so she went to the kitchen for her tea. When she got back the car was gone."

"Does she know what kind of a car it was?" Washington was eager.

Ohara sighed. "She doesn't know that, or the license number, only that the car was dark colored."

"Guess you can't expect bingo on the first card. What next?"

"It's still a working day—back to the office. We can't do much more here on this. We've got time for a quick lunch, though; how about a bowl of noodles?" Ohara looked at his companion and knew by his dismayed expression, unsuccessfully concealed, that a hamburger was the only lunch he craved. Smiling to himself, Ohara opened the car door. "Get in. There's a great little Japanese restaurant a few blocks from here. They make the best sushi and noodles I've ever had." As he started the car, he glanced at Washington's face, set in grim martyred lines, and laid it on. "Import all their fish from Japan."

They drove in silence until Washington managed a polite, "How did you discover this place?"

"I grew up around here. It's practically Japanese-town if you know where to look."

They drew up before an unpretentious cafe and went in. It had a simple bar counter and a few tables, strictly functional, but immaculately clean. The proprietor, his gray hair belied by the energy of his movements, was introduced as Tashimura-san. He fussed over Ohara like an old and valued friend. Washington perched on one of the stools at the counter and listened to the barrage of staccato Japanese. At last Ohara turned to him. "I ordered for you." He waited for the reaction but Washington refused to rise to the bait.

"Good!" he said, and waited grimly for lunch.

When it came, it was superb: a delicate soup, batter-fried shrimp that melted in the mouth, thick strips of steak in a

[30]

rich sauce, rice and salad. Ohara's lunch included a dish of sushi on the side.

When Washington had dispatched the shrimp and soup, and started on the steak, he looked over at Ohara. "I've got to admit it. I didn't want to come here, but this is real soul food. It's made a believer of me."

Ohara smiled. "Thought you'd like it. Tashimura's a good cook." He nodded at the old man whose gray head was just visible beyond the pass-through bar to the kitchen. "He'll remember you, and next time fix you something special."

"You seem to know him pretty well."

"Yes. He's an old friend of my family, from Manzanar days."

"Manzanar? Wasn't that the World War II Japanese confinement camp.? Always thought that was a pretty raw deal."

"Yes, pretty raw. Tashimura had a small grocery then and when he was sent to camp he had to sell everything to a speculator at two cents on the dollar. My dad had to leave his nursery; trees, plants, everything. He managed to keep the land, but the stock was left to rot. What didn't die was ripped off. I was only a little kid, but I remember my mom crying when some guy carted off her china and the little stuff she'd brought from Japan. Gave her ten bucks and said she was lucky to get it."

"Most people never heard about those things." Washington looked down at his plate, embarrassed. "I wonder if it would have made a difference if they had?"

Ohara shrugged. "I doubt it, in that kind of hysteria. There were a lot of stories like that."

"You people must have been pretty bitter." There was understanding on Washington's broad, black face.

"Some were," Ohara acknowledged. "But most were like my folks. When my dad came back from camp he worked as a gardener until he'd earned enough to start over. We tried to forget; it was simply something that had happened.

[31]

"A lot of our friends lost sons fighting with the American army in Europe. They thought of themselves as Americans, and raised their kids to be good Americans. We spoke English along with Japanese, ate as many hamburgers and fries as anybody else, went to American schools and colleges —became total Americans, except that we still looked Japanese."

Washington said nothing for a moment, understanding only too well what Ohara had left unsaid. He felt an empathy with him that wouldn't have seemed possible a few hours before.

"How did you come to join the force?" he asked at last.

"I thought about it a lot as a kid. The stories about Manzanar got to me. Maybe I wanted to prove something; I don't know." He glanced quickly at Washington, then continued in a lighter tone. "Anyway, I sure didn't want any part of the nursery business. I had to work too hard helping my dad. Then 'Nam came along. When I got back, I entered the police academy. Nothing else fitted."

Ohara stopped talking, wondering what there was about Washington that had led him to talk about things he usually kept to himself. Tashimura put a fresh pot of tea in front of them and some small bean jelly cakes. He thanked the old man. "How about you, Washington? Why are you a cop?"

"I grew up in Watts," Washington answered. "My dad was a night watchman for a TV factory. It was the dream of his life to be a cop, don't ask me why. But he didn't have the education. He kept drumming it into my head— stay in school, learn to be somebody. When I was fourteen he was killed by some punks who broke into the factory. One of them pulled a Saturday night special and shot him. That's when I decided to be a cop."

Ohara wondered if his decision had been an obligation or a choice. "Satisfied?" he asked.

"There's nothing else I want to do." For the first time, Washington smiled at him with the ease of understanding.

Ohara returned the smile. "Well, time to go. This one's on me."

Back at the office, Ohara had finished the court testimony notes and was rethinking the Smokey Trotter killing. He had not released to the newspapers the fact that it was not the beating, which lab tests showed had been done later, but a single practiced blow behind the ear that had killed Smokey. He'd just seen a man's hands, karate hands, that had been developed to maim and kill. Was there a connection?

His thinking was interrupted by a call from Fingerprints. When it was finished, he looked over at Ted Washington seated at the desk opposite, going over Reilly's files. "There's a make on the body. It's Roy Morgan, on parole from Folsom."

Washington whistled. "So much for the clean-cut college look."

"Call over to Records and have them send us Morgan's criminal file. Maybe the lab will have something, too."

Using the phone on his desk, Washington talked to Records. Before he had finished, Ohara had another call on his line. From the way he sat forward in his chair, it was obvious that something had happened. "Thanks, Bob," Ohara was saying. "I owe you. We're coming down now."

Washington was on his feet at once. This was more like it. "Where we going, boss man?"

"To the county morgue," Ohara answered, putting on his jacket. "We're going to poach a little on the Sheriff's territory. They've brought in a body from East L.A. with a stab wound almost identical to Morgan's."

VI

Bob Abrams, his beagle face anxious, was waiting for them just outside one of the autopsy rooms.

"I'm sticking my neck out for you, Sam," he said. "Hope you appreciate it. It's going to cost you one of Peggy's suki-yaki dinners."

"Done," Ohara agreed. "Now what have you got for me?"

"Come on." Abrams motioned for them to follow as he opened the door and went inside.

Washington, his stomach already queasy, was in no hurry to go along. Sensing his reluctance, Ohara touched him lightly on the arm. "All in a day's work, Ted."

"I know," Washington muttered. "I haven't been here since the academy, and I didn't like it then either."

Much to his relief, the actual autopsy had not yet been started. Morgan's body was on a table, bathed in the glow of the overhead lights like an actor in the wings waiting for his entrance.

Abrams pulled back the sheet. "We discovered this in the prelim." He raised one of the muscular arms and pointed beneath the armpit to a small tattoo of three intertwined sixes.

"So Morgan was Aryan Brotherhood," Ohara murmured.

Washington stared down at the triple-six tattoo, obscenely black against the death pallor of the soft flesh. "I've heard that has a biblical significance, but I don't know what."

"It's from Revelations." Ohara supplied the reference. "I believe the words go, 'The number of his name, six hundred three score and six, and no man might buy or sell save that he had the mark'—something like that." He bent over the body for a closer look at the wound.

Abrams pulled another wheeled table alongside. "This is what I wanted you to see." He pulled the sheet aside to expose the torso of a slightly built Chicano, whose Indian features had been sharpened by death into a stern nobility they could not have possessed in life. "Luis Lopez," Abrams read the name from a tag attached to the victim's toe. "It's Ed Baker's case, but it's so much like Morgan I thought you'd want a look-see."

The stab wound was in the same place as Morgan's. "In and out, slick as a whistle." Abrams gazed down with professional interest. "That was done by a pro, too."

"Yes," Ohara agreed, and went back to the table where Morgan's body lay. Washington's interest was overcoming his protesting stomach. He went from one body to the other, comparing the wounds. "Can you tell if it's the same weapon?"

"Not yet. When we go in I can tell more by the size and depth of the penetration."

Ohara noted that Morgan's wound was a little less "perfect," if it could be called that. He looked over at Abrams. "Anything of special interest in the Lopez report?"

"Not much. The body was found in a car behind a Chicano bar in East L.A."

Bending close to Morgan's body, Ohara pointed to the neck, where traces of abrasion showed. "Any idea what caused that?"

"Yes." Abrams went to a nearby table, picked up a glassine envelope and drew out a five-inch section of gold chain with a small charm hanging from the end. "This was caught under his shirt near the waistband. It either broke in the death struggle or was yanked off him. It scraped his neck in the process."

[36]

Ohara took the chain and held it under the light. The charm was a bicycle, attached to the chain by a flat disc of gold. The disc was engraved "K.C. 9.4.72."

"Can I take this?" he asked.

"Sure." Abrams handed him the glassine envelope. "Just sign for it." He went to a desk in the corner and brought back a form. While Ohara signed, Washington asked, "Was he a user?"

"No needle marks." Abrams came over to the table. "And his nose looks clean. I can tell you more when I open up the head." The queasy feeling returned to Ted's stomach.

"Looks like a nice clean kid," the ME went on, "at least according to his body. He sure took care of that."

Ohara joined them, studying Morgan's face. It was one Michelangelo might have copied for a marble angel. He wondered if there was anybody who would cry over him if they knew.

"OK, Bob," he said. "Thanks. Sukiyaki next week. I'll call you."

When they had left the room and headed for the elevator, Ted noted Ohara's thoughtful expression. "You thinking it's a gang job?"

"It could be," Ohara answered as the elevator enfolded them. "Adding the Lopez killing, it might be heading for an all-out gang war."

As they emerged from the elevator, a man hurried toward them. His sharp, nervous-looking face was intense with curiosity. "Talk to you a minute, Ohara? I'm Leo Krepp—maybe you remember, interviewed you a few weeks ago on a case—"

Ohara remembered the inquisition only too well. "Yes?"

"I'm doing a feature news series on the increase of crime in L.A., my specialty, you know. Anything new on The Oleander Murder?"

"What murder?"

"Hell, the information office said the guy's name was Roy Morgan, but it'll be The Oleander Murder in my series, more pizzazz."

"There's nothing for the papers just yet."

"Oh, come off it. You wouldn't be down here after hours if there wasn't, so give."

"Sorry, no comment." Ohara flung out the hackneyed phrase and resumed walking toward the door. Krepp tagged along beside them, nervously running his fingers through his stringy red hair.

"Look, I've been covering this from the beginning. I got a tip that this Lopez the Sheriff's brought in was stabbed in the same way as Morgan and in the same place. You've got to know that's a gang-style stabbing. What's the tie-in with Morgan?"

Ohara and Washington kept walking. "Can't say yet."

Krepp followed them down the steps and up to their car. "Come on, you can give me something."

"Nothing. Sorry." Ohara opened the car door and got in. Washington shouldered Krepp aside, entered the car and slammed the door.

"Up you, Ohara-san, play it close. I've got other sources."

As they pulled away from the curb into traffic, Washington looked back to see Krepp's lanky figure hurrying back up the steps into the morgue. "Who does that guy think he is?"

"He's a freelance who thinks he's an investigative reporter. He goes for the sensational stuff just often enough to have a following. Bucking for a Pulitzer I guess."

"That'll be the day. Well, where to now?"

"I'm going home. Want me to drop you at the station?"

"Yes. My car's there. Anything more tonight?"

"No."

"Good. I've got plans—about five-foot-three and stacked."

Washington smiled appreciatively as his hands described the form of an imaginary hourglass.

"Young and single!" Ohara grinned over at him. "I can't even remember that far back."

Despite his remark about Washington's enviable single status, Ohara was looking forward to the pleasant normality of an evening at home with the family. The freeway traffic was bad as usual, so it was almost eight by the time he pulled into his driveway. Amplified guitars booming from the neighboring garage told him that Jim, his son, was rehearsing with the Seven Samurai next door. With eardrums anticipating the blessed quiet of the house, he unlocked the door and went in. "Peggy, I'm home—"

There was no answering welcome. Disappointed, he remembered. It was Peggy's night to teach a self-defense class at the community center. Suzy, his daughter, was as usual watching her favorite TV program in the den. He entered unnoticed. "How's my girl?" he asked, distracting her with a quick kiss.

"Oh, Daddy, you're home." She returned her attention to the TV screen. "Mom said to tell you dinner's in the oven and salad in the refrigerator." He stood a moment watching, just to be with her, then left to change into comfortable slacks and tee-shirt.

The dinner in the oven was home-cooked and good. As he sat down to his lonely meal, however, he recalled a book someone had given him about a fictional Japanese detective whose efforts were aided, or soothed, as the case might be, by frequent dips in a steaming hot *ofuro*, while his beautiful Japanese wife, elegantly kimonoed, waited nearby with fragrant tea and fluffy white towels. Only in books, he reflected wryly.

Though he missed Peggy's welcoming kiss and the way

[39]

she made coming home special, he couldn't begrudge her the activities she enjoyed. Somehow, Peggy and he had survived the strain of his irregular hours, which brought about such things as aborted plans, disappointed kids and lonely evenings. They made the most of what time they had together. He was lucky; marriage casualties among police were almost an occupational certainty. It took a dedicated, loving woman to marry a cop.

Peggy's way of coping had been the community center and going back to college after the kids were old enough. She kept her family tight-knit with old-fashioned Japanese skill. At five-foot-one, she'd never be elegant, kimonoed or otherwise, but she fitted his arms and filled his heart.

Dinner finished, he stacked the dishes and settled himself in the living room with a book. He'd been reading about twenty minutes when the phone rang.

As he'd guessed, it was the station: armed robbery of a jade collection, prominent citizens. Normally, Vince Scott would handle it, but he was out sick and his partner Yost was in San Francisco on a murder case follow-up. Ohara hung up and dialed Washington's number. It took several rings before the phone was answered.

"I don't believe it," Washington grumbled. "You don't know what I've got here—I've worked on this for weeks."

"Sorry, Ted." Ohara meant it; he'd been through it himself. "That's why you get more money in Detectives."

"I knew there had to be a catch somewhere." Washington's gloom was thick enough to cut.

"Maybe she'll wait."

"Maybe I'll win the Irish Sweepstakes."

"It's happened before." Ohara pulled it together. "Pick me up at my place, Ted. I'll be waiting."

It was well after midnight by the time they'd finished the preliminary investigation and had reassured the frightened victims. Vince Scott, they hoped, would take over by morning.

Washington drove back to Ohara's place with amazing speed. "We might as well have used a red light and siren," Ohara said as he got out of the car. "You in a hurry?"

"Damn right. I sold her on watching the late show. I just hope it was long enough."

Ohara gave a thumbs-up gesture as Washington pulled away. When he let himself into the house, it was dark except for a small lamp in the living room. He'd hoped that Peggy might still be awake, but there was no sound from the bedroom. He had a cold beer, then went into the bedroom to undress. Peggy could sleep through a tornado, he thought, as he finally lay down beside her. He sighed and touched her fingers lightly by way of goodnight.

"Isamu," she murmured drowsily and moved against him.

Ohara gathered her close, enjoying the softness of her hair against his cheek. "A fine Japanese wife you are," he teased. "Why isn't my *ofuro* steaming? Why aren't you waiting with the fluffy white towels and hot tea I've read about? I've a mind to send you back to *Ojiisan*. Your grandfather should have taught you better."

"Would you really send me back, *donasama*, father of my children?" Her lips brushed his provocatively.

"Well, maybe not this time," he said. With the very best of Zen, Ohara closed his mind to everything but the present moment.

VII

THE next morning Ohara woke to teasing aromas from the kitchen. Peggy hadn't forgotten it was a court day. She knew how he disliked them and always made something special for breakfast. When he entered the kitchen she was busy at the stove, trim in white slacks and red cotton top. He folded his arms around her and kissed her neck. "Kids gone already?"

"Yes." She smiled up at him. "Jim left early for his new job. Suzy went to the beach with Kathy Ozawa."

Ohara sat down and picked up his juice.

"Ready in a minute, Isamu." Peggy always called him by his Japanese name when she felt particularly affectionate.

He watched her as she buttered toast, poured the coffee, dished up a puffy golden omelette. Her movements had the unobtrusive grace peculiar to so many Japanese women. The years seemed barely to have touched her. Her face, framed by short curly hair, was young, her skin velvet smooth. She could still be proud of her figure, girl-slim after two children and several years of marriage. In fact, she looked almost the same as the day they'd met at her grandfather's Aikido *dojo*.

Ohara smiled, remembering how miffed he'd been when a slim, undersized girl had presented herself as his partner. It had dented his ego to find out that Master Takahashi thought he was no better than that.

But when she'd bowed and proceeded to toss him head over heels with an effortless flick of her wrist, he'd learned better. He'd sat dumbfounded on the *tatami* thinking what a pretty girl she was. Then she'd put her hand before her mouth, Japanese fashion, to cover the giggle she couldn't restrain. "Want to try it again?"

It had taken several hundred falls before she'd agreed to marry him.

Peggy brought him back to the present as she set his plate before him. "*Ohio goazimasu, donasama*," she said, her eyes demurely downcast. "Humble wife would inquire if you have rested well?" Her aspect of wifely submission was somewhat marred by the smile twitching her lips.

Ohara reached over, swatted her round little rear and joined the game. "*Hai*, mighty *donasama*, father of your children, has rested well."

He took a bite of the omelette and sighed appreciatively. "I've decided to keep you, wife. You may forget the finer points of caring for a Japanese husband, but you have other qualities I can't resist."

"I thought you'd remember," she said and kissed him, not at all demurely.

When he was on his second cup of coffee, he picked up the newspaper. A headline caught his eye: *The Oleander Murder*. It was a feature treatment of the Morgan case by Leo Krepp, and referred to the Lopez killing as well, hinting at a connection between the two. Krepp's conclusion was dramatic and ominous. "Are prison gangs waging war in our streets, endangering our citizens? Are police playing down the truth? Lieutenant Sam Ohara, investigator on The Oleander Murder, refused to talk to this reporter. We wonder why."

Ohara threw down the paper and stood up, the euphoric mood of the morning shattered. "Time I got going," he said, not wanting his irritation to spill over on to Peggy. He knew that Leo Krepp's article was going to make trouble for him. Considerable trouble.

The court case was prolonged and he was kept waiting over three hours before his testimony was required. Then the defense counsel chewed over each and every point like a terrier with a bone. When Ohara was finally excused it was mid-afternoon. He headed for the office.

A report on Washington's interview with Morgan's parole officer lay on his desk, along with the license number of Morgan's car. There was also a note that Ted had gone to interview Morgan's employer at Mort's Garage. Ohara settled down to read the report, pleased that his new assistant had been busy and effective.

According to the parole officer, Morgan apparently had been playing it straight. He'd made his appointments on time, stayed out of trouble, and held a part-time job at the garage. The next step would be to go to Morgan's apartment. Ohara was about to leave when his phone rang.

"The captain would like to see you in his office." The brief message made Ohara's stomach tighten. When Captain Krauss wanted to see anyone, it usually meant he was unhappy. Gerhard Krauss unhappy was not something to be taken lightly.

When he entered the captain's office, the morning newspaper was on the desk, spread open to Krepp's story. "Sit down, Sam." The captain flashed a brief, humorless smile and pointed to the newspaper. "What's this about—this 'Oleander Murder'?"

"Just Krepp waxing lyrical over the Morgan case."

"Do you think there's a gang tie-in?"

"It's possible."

"Did you give Krepp this information?"

"No."

"I don't like this implication of a police cover-up. Did you provoke it?"

"Definitely not. He wanted a story I couldn't give him so he made it a personal issue."

The desk lamp shone across Krauss's heavy round face,

giving it a severity that belied his Santa Claus appearance. "Fill me in."

"The two murders could be gang-related, but a couple of things don't fit." Ohara stopped there, not sure he could justify to Krauss's pragmatic reasoning why an oleander petal and a gold charm were nudging him in another direction. Krauss detested speculation. "As soon as I've checked both cases I can be more definite."

The intercom buzzed on Krauss's desk. He pushed the button and said, "Hold." Krauss knew Sam Ohara was good; he'd give him a little more time and to hell with Krepp. "Well, get a move on, Sam. This is going to stir up the media, and you'd better not leave us with egg on our faces."

Krauss turned back to the paperwork on his desk after waving one pudgy hand in dismissal. It was one of his less endearing qualities that he tended to give orders like his stiff-necked Prussian ancestors. Ohara resented the touch of the whip, but he kept his control in place out of respect for the fact that, despite his heavy-handed manner, Krauss was a good and dedicated cop. He stayed seated. "Anything else?"

Krauss looked up with a frown. "No." He gave no indication of his inner amusement. He might have known Ohara wouldn't be hurried or curtly dismissed—too damn much Japanese pride.

When Ohara was almost to the door, Krauss stopped him. "You always do a good job, Sam. You're careful and that's good in my book. Just do this one before Krepp's pressure cooker explodes and a lot of people get burned."

Ohara recognized the unspoken apology. "I know, but jumping on that kind of bandwagon could fire up a full-scale gang war. Suppose Krepp is wrong?"

Krauss nodded, his face grave as he watched Ohara leave.

There was a visitor waiting for Ohara when he reached his office. The man stood up. "Sam O'Hara?"

"Yes. What can I do for you?" His visitor looked surprised but held out his hand. "I'm Ed Baker, Sheriff's."

Ohara knew Baker only by reputation, but he could see that reality outdid rumor. Baker was a big, tough cop, and it was obvious that he worked at looking that way. His shoulders and arms shouted "muscle," his tightly cinched belt underlined restraint. A brown mustache framed firm lips, and his gray eyes showed a sudden wariness as he studied the Japanese.

"You're the damndest Irishman I've ever seen."

Amusement lit Ohara's face. "It affects a lot of people that way. But Ohara is a good old Japanese name, too. We just spell it differently."

The big man accepted this with a grin. "Bet they rub your nose in it."

"True." Ohara liked Baker's frank manner. "Sit down. What's on your mind?"

"This is what I wanted to talk about." He laid Krepp's article on the desk. "Seen it?"

"I've seen it." Ohara's expression was pained. "So has the captain."

Baker smiled. "My sympathy. But it looks like Krepp has hit it right on. Have you seen Lopez's body?"

"Yesterday at the morgue. The wounds look similar."

"The gang tie-in's there. Morgan's got an Aryan Brotherhood tattoo." Baker looked pleased.

"How about Lopez?"

"He's been on our books a long time. He's a Mexican Mafia soldier."

Ohara sighed. "I hate to think Krepp may be right, but it's

[47]

going together like a jigsaw puzzle. If it is a gang fight, it started with the Smokey Trotter killing. He's Black Guerrilla Family. I can't prove it yet—but Morgan probably did it. He was karate trained—hard style, that's how Trotter was killed."

Baker leaned forward. "Maybe I can give you another piece of the puzzle. I know that stabbing MO, and the bastard that uses it. Name's Lucky Montero, 'Triple A Lucky.' We've had him pegged for more than one stabbing with everything but stand-up evidence. He's always managed to cover his ass."

"Freelance hit man?"

"Nope. Nuestra Familia brass, a captain. I think it shapes up this way. Smokey, a big man in the Black Guerrilla Family, was snuffed by Morgan for the Brotherhood. So the Black Guerrilla Family asks their allies, Nuestra Familia, to take out Morgan."

"Why not do it themselves?"

"Maybe they had a favor coming. Maybe they wanted to be sure of their friends in case things got hot."

"And Lopez?"

"He could have heard something. Montero doesn't leave any loose ends. What do you think?"

"It's a real can of worms," Ohara said noncommittally. "Can you get Montero on the Lopez killing?"

"No." Baker looked deflated. "It's the same old story. He and his brother came into the bar where Lopez was drinking, but left about twenty minutes before the victim. The Monteros were seen driving away. When the bar closed, several hours later, the owner found Lopez's body in his car in the parking lot in back. When we checked out Montero, his brother and two friends swore he'd spent the evening with them. That's damn hard to break."

"So far I've no connection between Montero and Morgan."

[48]

Ohara knew he wasn't making points with Baker, but fact was fact.

"Suppose I give you a couple?" Baker pressed. "First, there's the gang alliance, right? Second, Montero came to town the day before Morgan was killed. One of our boys spotted him at the airport. His brother met him so they probably went to his place in Brentwood."

"His brother tied in too?"

Baker shrugged. "So far his nose is clean. His money is supposed to have come from investments."

"Is Montero there now?"

"No, he entered the hospital this morning for minor surgery. If we could sweat him on the Morgan killing, he might not be so lucky with his alibi. He doesn't know he's a suspect on that one."

"I'd need more than that even to question him."

"Let me see the file on Morgan. Maybe I can spot a tie-in."

Ohara gave Baker the file. He read it carefully, but handed it back, disappointed. "Nothing there."

"I've got some more checking to do," Ohara said. "I'll keep Montero in mind and if I find anything at all I'll be in touch."

"I'll trace Montero's movements on the day of Morgan's killing. That might give us something concrete."

When Baker left, Ohara sat down at his desk and picked up the glassine envelope with the pink oleander petal that had clung to Morgan's bare chest. It didn't fit into the scenario of a Mafia hit man, but it belonged to Morgan's last hours and was still unexplained.

"Hi! You look like you could use a violin." Washington's deep voice scattered his thoughts.

"A violin?" Ohara stared blankly at him.

"That's the approved Holmes technique, isn't it?"

Ohara laughed. There were depths to Washington he hadn't

guessed. "I've a feeling the captain would frown on violins and cocaine. By the way, the case has a name—The Oleander Murder—christened by Krepp in the morning paper."

"I saw the piece." Washington's face showed his distaste. "Who was that just leaving the office?"

"Baker, from Sheriff's. He has some ideas on the case."

"Can he prove anything?"

"No, but it's the best lead we've got so far—a Nuestra Familia hit man who uses that particular stabbing MO."

"Where do we come in?"

"Right now, doing our own thing. We're going to check out Morgan's apartment. On the way there you can fill me in on what you turned up today."

VIII

MORGAN'S apartment was in Glendale. Ohara drove and Washington settled back to relax while he could. He'd had a busy morning. It was gratifying to hear Ohara say, "That was a good job you did this morning, Ted. Appreciate it. What did you find out from the garage where Morgan worked?"

Washington forgot he was tired; he'd been waiting to spring this bit of work. "Morgan was employed there all right, but not regularly. He specialized in foreign cars. The owner said he believed in giving ex-cons a chance, but I don't buy him as a guy who'd give anyone the shell of an egg if he didn't have to."

Ohara laughed. "That shell of an egg bit is good."

"It's my mother's. She has maxims and sayings to fit every situation. Anyway, I checked back with the parole officer. Mort's Garage hired Morgan on the first interview, as they had one or two others. But not everybody the parole officer sent over there for a job got one, qualified or not. Only whites were hired."

"Sounds about as straight as a four-cornered egg, as my Uncle Ushiro would say."

"Mama would like that one. I must remember to tell her."

Ohara looked thoughful. "So, could be Mort's Garage is a Brotherhood operation, sponsoring useful Brothers to satisfy parole requirements while they go about more important business elsewhere."

"Maybe Morgan's business was to pick up Smokey Trotter's clientele, one way or another."

"Sharp boy! The Black Guerrilla Family wouldn't like that." Then Ohara told him Baker's theory on Lucky Montero.

Before long they turned off Brand Boulevard into a neighborhood of frame and concrete bungalows. They made another turn and the bungalows gave way to a new development of singles apartments. Sandwiched between Exotic Hawaii and Historic Tudor was Old Spain. The number on its wrought-iron gates was Morgan's address.

In the entrance foyer a discreet sign informed, "Manager, Apt. 10." As they walked past the red-tiled fountain and the landscaped pool, Washington sighed. "Just look what I've been missing all these years in my efficiency apartment."

"Don't give up your lease," Ohara cautioned. "You probably couldn't afford this—neither could I."

"How could Morgan, on a part-time garage mechanic's salary?"

"Good question." Ohara smiled without humor. "Maybe he did a little moonlighting on the side."

Three tiled steps leading through an opulent stone archway dropped them in front of Apartment 10. An unobtrusive black and gold sign said, "C. Leibman, Manager."

C. Leibman, when she answered the door, did not go with the lush Old World decor. She was lean and tanned as an old pocketbook, with a bleached Orphan Annie hairdo and shrewd gray eyes that surveyed them coldly. "Yes?" Her voice with its drill sergeant's overtones sounded as if she'd rather say no.

Ohara smiled, turning up the wattage just enough to thaw the frost, then produced his ID. "You are Miss Leibman, the manager?" She nodded, looking annoyed. "We'd like to talk to you for a few minutes. You might be able to help us in our investigation."

As she studied Ohara her eyes grew bedroom warm. She hadn't guessed Japanese men had that kind of sex appeal. Her acquaintance with the genre had been limited to the heavyset gardener across the street; this one was something else. "I'd be happy to help, if I can. Do come in." Her smile gave its own invitation as she held the door open. It was all for Ohara. Her red-tipped fingers just brushed his sleeve as she ushered them inside.

"Would you like coffee, or something else?" She nodded playfully in the direction of a small bar against the wall.

"Thank you, no, but it's kind of you to offer. We'd like to ask you about one of your tenants, Roy Morgan."

Her smile diminished. "I don't know what I could possibly tell you, officer. I make it a rule not to pry into my tenants' affairs. As long as they pay their rent on time and there's no disturbance, I feel they're entitled to their privacy. Mr. Morgan was a good tenant, that's all I know."

"He's been murdered, ma'am," Washington said flatly. "Anything you tell us can't hurt him now, but it may help us find out who killed him."

Shock cracked her careful facade. She looked suddenly old and afraid. "Not Roy? I can't believe it! When did it happen?"

"The day before yesterday," Ohara replied, watching her face. "It was in the papers."

"Oh, I never read the papers—the news is always so dreadful." She folded her arms around her thin body as if for warmth. "Why—he was such a nice boy, always so helpful, bringing me little presents." She caught her lip between her teeth and looked unseeing at the carpet.

"When did you see him last, Miss Leibman?" Ohara sounded like a sympathetic friend.

"Why, I saw him just about four o'clock—I guess it was the day before yesterday. I was at the pool and he waved to me as he went out. I just can't believe—" She broke off and shivered. "God, I've got to have a drink."

They waited while she poured herself a scotch, took a quick gulp and set the glass down with an unsteady hand.

"We'd like to see his apartment," Ohara said gently.

She looked startled. "Oh, yes, I suppose you have to..." Going to a desk in the corner she took a set of keys from a drawer. When she turned to face them her mind was already turning from sadness to more practical matters. "I do hope you won't have to disturb the other tenants. Thank heaven you're not in uniform."

Without speaking further she led the way to Morgan's apartment, which was at the end of the columned cloister. She selected a key, inserted it and turned the knob. "Oh, my God!"

The door had opened onto a shambles—furniture ripped apart, pictures yanked from the walls, the contents of drawers and cupboards scattered on the floor. They went inside and through the bedroom door saw mattress and bedding upended in a heap, the bed pulled away from the wall.

"Oh, this is terrible—terrible!" The woman's hand went to her heart; with sudden concern Washington eased her into a chair.

Ohara made a quick check of the other rooms. "Come and gone," he said when he returned. "I'll need to use the phone in your apartment, Miss Leibman." She nodded weakly. "Stay with her, Ted. I'll be right back."

When Ohara returned she'd revived enough to be vocal about her distress. Washington, looking strained, was listening stoically to her complaints. Much to his relief, Ohara took over.

"This has been a bad shock for you, I know. But I wonder if you could do one more thing for us? After that we'll let you go back to your apartment to rest. Will you show Mr. Washington the garage where Roy Morgan parked his car? I'll take care of things here."

She responded to his touch and warmed herself at his

concern. "Yes, of course, then I must rest, you're right." With a last pathetic smile for Ohara, she rose and followed Washington out of the room.

That problem disposed of, Ohara began a meticulous survey of the wrecked apartment without disturbing anything the lab would need to see. Whoever had done the job had forced a kitchen window, which faced onto the parking alley. The medicine cabinet had been ransacked. He was examining a dusting of white powder on the deep blue rug beside the bed when he heard Washington come back. "In here, Ted."

Washington joined him in the bedroom. "Morgan's car is not in the garage. I'll put out a bulletin on it."

Ohara nodded agreement, then pointed to the powder-stained rug. "Look at this—there's a little more near the head of the bed."

The faint white trail led behind the pulled-out bed to where a gaping hole marred the pale cream symmetry of the wall. It was empty of the light socket it should have contained. Ohara bent down for a closer look. A minute scrap of plastic was stuck on the edge of the hole.

Washington sucked in his breath. "If that's what I think it is, we know what kind of moonlighting Morgan did. No wonder he could afford to live here."

Ohara straightened. "If Morgan was dealing for the Brotherhood, they wouldn't want competition from Smokey Trotter. It makes Baker's theory look a lot better. Reilly's narcotics informants say Smokey had Black Guerrilla Family backing for his dealership. They wouldn't let his killing go—not if they want to stay on top."

"The Morgan stabbing isn't their style, though," Washington objected as he followed Ohara into the other room.

"According to Baker, that's where Lucky Montero fits in.

The Black Guerrilla Family borrowed him from Nuestra Familia to keep the local noses clean. He comes, does the job, goes."

"Possible," Washington agreed, then was silent a minute. "Sam, maybe I should hit the streets and see if I can get something solid to tie it up."

The offer surprised Ohara, but he saw its value. "It's what we need all right, but it's dangerous. We might be able to get it from the narcs."

Washington shook his head. "Not fast enough. I know what we need, and more important, I know how to talk to the brothers and sisters. My undercover stint as a flaky black from Chicago was pretty good."

"Where did you work it?"

"Anaheim, Torrance, Whittier."

Ohara saw the confidence in Ted's broad, determined face. "OK, Ted. You've got it, but coordinate with Reilly and keep in touch with me. When will you start?"

"Tonight. So if you don't need me here, I'd like to get rolling."

There was a knock at the door. "Probably the lab crew," Ohara said, and they went together to open it.

As the specialists filed in with their equipment, Ohara touched Washington on the shoulder. "Be careful, Ted." He looked at him for a moment, then smiled. "After all, the case is too far along to break in anybody else."

"I'll remember that," Washington said, and was on his way. Ohara watched him go, not liking the odds but knowing the idea was sound and the need urgent.

As he waited for the lab crew to finish, Ohara went over to an impressive-looking desk in one corner of the living room. Its scattered papers proved uninformative, but the telephone Yellow Pages lay open, undisturbed, at the section on jewelers. One ad for a Burbank firm was checked in pencil.

The ad copy said they specialized in trophies and had a unique selection of charms and pendants. He thought about the gold charm taken from Morgan's body and made a note of the address.

The leather wastebasket beside the desk held an old newspaper. It was dated the day Morgan had been killed, and was folded back to the sixth page. Scanning it he found a short paragraph about the Smokey Trotter killing at the bottom of the page. He put the paper down and looked into the wastebasket once more.

It was empty except for a broken Japanese doll. Ohara reached in and picked out the pieces—the torso in a kimono of fine red silk and the head, which had been snapped off. He fitted the small damaged head onto the jagged break of the neck.

Whoever had made the doll was an artist. The face was extremely well done, with personality and expression in every finely drawn line. The kimono was exquisitely detailed. It was the kind of doll to keep in a case. How had Morgan come by it?

It was a pity to see such a perfect little work of art destroyed. The innocent doll face smiled up at him as he stroked the silky black hair. "Where did you come from, *Akachan?*"

The puzzle intrigued him—a broken doll, a specialty jeweler's address, a pink oleander petal, and a gold bicycle charm on a piece of broken chain.

IX

WHILE waiting for the technical crew to finish, Ohara sat back and thought. From the evidence thus far, he could jump on his horse and ride off in all directions. He smiled as the old joke came to mind; it fitted his predicament exactly. The broken chain with its date-engraved charm, the doll and the jeweler's ad, all directly related to Morgan, pointed one way. The destructive search of Morgan's apartment suggested simple murder for gain, with drug-related suspects. A gang vendetta was still another way to go.

He wanted to talk to Abrams again before pursuing the gang angle involving Montero. The technicians should be finished in another ten minutes; then he would go over to the morgue.

When Ohara finally arrived at the morgue, Abrams had just finished a long series of tests and was ready for a coffee break. Together they went to the canteen and settled at a corner table with coffee and a couple of doughnuts.

"You don't usually buy me coffee, Sam, so what's on your mind?"

Ohara took a sip of his black coffee and watched Abrams begin to demolish a doughnut. "The Morgan-Lopez connection. Now that you've had a further look, how nearly identical were the wounds?"

"Amazingly similar. Same place, same stiletto-type blade, same angle of left-handed thrust from behind."

"What I'm really asking, I guess, is what are the differences?"

Abrams wiped powdered sugar off his fingers. "The wound measurements are almost identical. But I had the feeling there might be a difference in the weight of the weapon, or the force of the thrust."

Interested, Ohara pulled on the small thread of difference. "In which case was it stronger, or heavier?"

"Lopez, I'd say. In both cases the thrust penetrated to the aorta, but in Morgan the point of entry was imperfect, as if it wasn't a sure stroke. Maybe he turned or jerked at the last minute."

"Different weapons?"

Abrams considered that. "It's possible, but to be honest, I'm just guessing. I can't hand you hard proof." Bob took another swallow of coffee and reached for the second doughnut.

"Baker thinks the same man did both murders." Ohara watched for Abrams's reaction. The ME shrugged. "It's logical, but I take it you don't."

Ohara pushed his coffee aside. "He could be right, but I'm just not satisfied." He explained the latest developments. "The apartment manager saw him at about four P.M. Does that narrow the time of death much?"

Abrams nodded. "The stomach was almost empty, so he hadn't eaten dinner. Following normal patterns, that would put it between five and eight P.M."

"It gives me a time frame to check."

"Got a suspect?"

"According to Baker, it was a Nuestra Familia hit man's MO on both the killings. That's why I think the differences are important. We're getting pressure on the gang issue. A gang hit would be a welcome solution in a lot of quarters."

Abrams leaned back in his chair. "Guesses and possibilities, Sam—what you need is a new fortune cookie. It's a bitch of a case."

The next morning Krepp's column drew a grim picture of the prison gang power struggle for control of the drug traffic on the outside. A shot of Lopez's funeral and one of Morgan's body were captioned, "Gang War Victims—Who's Next?" His windup was dramatic: "The public should be told just how far the gang influence extends. A well-known gang figure was questioned in regard to the Lopez murder, but he is still at liberty. We think he should be questioned in the Morgan killing, but has he? The police are usually quite efficient in these matters. Why not this time?"

Ohara read it, and wondered if Krepp realized he might be buying himself a load of trouble.

Captain Krauss, absent from the city, missed the story, so his ulcer was able to rest in peace.

Yumi's mother, alone in the grocery, read the column through twice. For the first time, Hana Kubota felt the shadow of fear lighten. After that terrible night, she'd waited for the blow to fall, like someone condemned. She had lain awake nights going over and over everything she'd done, looking for mistakes that would bring the police to her door. But praise Buddha, Yumi seemed to have survived the ordeal better than she could have hoped. Thanks in part to the medicine Hana had given her, Yumi had slept for fourteen hours. Then, when she'd awakened, the horror seemed to have been washed from her mind.

But Hana could not forget. She was haunted by the remembrance of what she'd had to do. If she hadn't gone home that day because of old Mrs. Hata—she shut her mind against the thought. Even in the morning sunshine, she shivered. She'd saved Yumi and Kenji; that was all that mattered. To reassure herself she read the column again, then carefully shredded the page and dropped it in the wastebasket. Yumi must never see the man's picture.

When he arrived at the station, Ohara checked the other newspapers. So far they hadn't followed Krepp's lead. He wondered how long they would hold off.

He called Reilly in Narcotics, but there had been no word

from Ted Washington since he'd checked with them yesterday.

Next he dialed the East Los Angeles Sheriff's station and got Ed Baker. "Anything more on Montero?"

"No," Baker answered. "I tried to check his movements on the day Morgan was killed. He seems to have just dropped out of sight."

"Where is he now?"

"He's left the hospital to recuperate at his brother's place in Brentwood."

"Maybe we should go visit the sick."

"That's what I was thinking. When?"

"Say, three o'clock. Give me the address; I'll meet you out front."

Ohara had no sooner hung up than the phone rang. It was Abrams at the morgue. "Sam, Morgan's father has come to claim his body. Said he'd read about his son's death in the papers. Any reason not to release the body?"

"No, but think up a little red tape until I get there. I want to talk to him."

When Ohara reached the morgue waiting room, he stood a moment at the door, studying the man in a neat dark suit sitting by the window. Morgan's father seemed unaware of his surroundings, which attempted with plastic cheerfulness to deny their proximity to death.

Ohara went up to him and held out his hand. "Mr. Morgan? I'm Detective Ohara, in charge of your son's case."

The man stood up and shook hands. There was no sense of greeting. It was a gesture only, of automatic ingrained respect for all officialdom. "Can I call the undertaker now? I want to take Roy home."

"In just a few more minutes," Ohara said gently. "I'd like to ask you some questions. It might help me find the person who did this to your son."

Resignedly, the man sat down again. Ohara took the chair beside him. "Not much to tell, officer."

He seemed unable to go on, so Ohara helped him. "Where's your home, Mr. Morgan?"

"We have a little farm just outside of King City. That's why I didn't hear about Roy sooner. We don't get a paper." He hesitated, then went on. "A neighbor saw Roy's picture in the paper and told us."

Ohara couldn't help thinking what a shock that must have been. But then, however that kind of news comes, it's a shock. "When was the last time you saw your son?"

"Summer of seventy-two, August." Morgan looked down at his hands, gripping each other until the knuckles whitened. "Roy hated our farm. He was always getting into some kind of trouble in school. Started staying away from home, running with a bad crowd in King City. One day I told him he'd have to straighten out or get out, because he was breaking his mother's heart."

Morgan stopped speaking for a moment, then went doggedly on. "Roy just laughed and said, 'You bet I'll get out. I'm not going to end up like you.'" The pain of remembering was vivid in the old man's face.

Ohara didn't interrupt. The information was of no immediate help, but he sensed how much Morgan needed to talk.

"I thought he'd learn his lesson and come home again, but he didn't. Mother wouldn't rest until I went to look for him in the city. I never found him. Later on we got a letter from him—from prison, asking for money for cigarettes." Morgan reached for a handkerchief from his back pocket and wiped his eyes. "I just couldn't bring myself to answer it. Wish now I had. Maybe it would have made all the difference."

[63]

He looked over at Ohara. The expression in his eyes was tragic. "Officer, did I kill my boy? When I threw him out—you know, it was just to make him realize—I never really meant—"

Ohara spoke quickly. "No, Mr. Morgan. You didn't kill Roy. The life he chose killed him. Put anything else out of your mind!" His dark eyes held the old man's for a moment in a concentrated mental effort to replace the torturing self-doubt with acceptance and peace.

Slowly, Morgan's hands relaxed. "I believe you, officer. Thank you."

After a moment Ohara stood up. "I've no more questions, sir. I'll take you down to the office and you can make the arrangements to take your son home."

When he left Morgan carefully signing the forms that would give him back his son's body, Ohara realized, as he had so often before, that there is seldom only one victim. He was still moved by the personal tragedies that became the routine statistics of his job.

X

WHEN Ohara returned to the station, he hoped for a report from Washington, but there was nothing except a message that Sergeant Baker from Sheriff's had been trying to reach him.

He telephoned Baker, whose news was bad. "We're busted, Ohara." Baker's frustration showed in his voice. "Montero was in the hospital for a preoperative checkup from noon until seven-thirty on the day Morgan was killed. He was seen in the East L.A. bar at eight, left at half past eight, and is alibied by his brother and two other witnesses from nine o'clock on."

"It looked good, too." Ohara knew only too well how Baker felt.

"We even pressed the brother on the new time frame. He said he was 'glad to help'; gave me the doctor's name, the floor nurse, the hospital room number, the whole bit. He really enjoyed himself. It all checks out."

"It's almost too good, but I guess that tears it."

"Yeah, Lucky's screwed us again. But I'm gonna work on that alibi for Lopez."

"Something might turn up. And Ed, thanks for all the help."

Ohara sat back in his chair, feeling deflated. The Montero lead had been close to a probable. But until he had something more definite on Morgan, he still couldn't rule out gang vengeance. What's more, he could rely on Krepp to fan the flames. Now he'd have to start over again with no preconceived premise.

Resorting to an Aikido technique that always worked, he

let his breathing slow and deepen as he sat motionless, with half-closed eyes. Each exhaled breath took with it patterned thought and awareness of time, until his body felt light and his mind was clear. Then he went back to the beginning—the pink oleander petal clinging to Morgan's bloodied chest. It was a pointer to where he'd been killed, but California's prolific growth of pink and white oleander bushes made it a discouraging lead.

The next piece of concrete evidence was the bicycle charm. He took it out of his desk and held it in his hand. The engraved notation looked simple. Was "K.C." someone's initials? The "9.4.72" was almost certainly a date.

Ohara got out Morgan's file. The rap sheet was a classic progress profile from juvenile delinquency to habitual criminal. He'd done his hard time in Folsom, sentenced in 1976, paroled in 1978. Near the bottom of the page was a notation that Morgan, along with several others, had been questioned and released in connection with the rape-murder of an eleven-year-old girl, September—Ohara turned the page then stared at the words—King City. He looked down at the letters "K.C." on the charm. Morgan had been raised just outside King City; his father had said the boy left home in August 1972. Ohara reached for the telephone.

The King City police promised to send a copy of the case record. It was past history, but it could be relevant to Morgan's murder. Nothing else in the file had so roused Ohara's hunting instincts.

He also had the marked jeweler's ad he'd found on Morgan's desk. It was a good time to check it out. From there he could go to Shimizu's doll shop in Little Tokyo to inquire about the doll. He found a large manila envelope, dropped the broken doll inside and took it along.

When he arrived at the jewelry store, an elderly man laid aside the innards of a watch he had been adjusting and greeted his customer. Ohara identified himself and asked if the jeweler had recently had an order from a Roy Morgan for a gold charm.

The man replied that he had just had a rush order for a gold charm come in and the name might be Morgan; he would check. He disappeared behind a partition, then came back with a small envelope on which the name Morgan was written. "Finished job came in this morning, officer," he said as he pulled over a square velvet pad. Opening the flap of the envelope, he let a gold charm slide out onto the soft surface.

Ohara picked it up. It was a gold teddy bear with an attached circle for hanging on a chain. Turning it over he found, as he'd expected, that it was engraved "L.A. 8.5.83." His excitement quickened. That was the date Morgan had been killed. "Can you tell me when this order was brought in?"

The man nodded. "Yes, happens I can. I was alone in the shop and took the order myself. That's my writing on the slip. It was late last Thursday."

"Was Mr. Morgan alone?"

"Yes. He was such a pleasant young man, clean-cut, not like so many nowadays. He asked specifically for a teddy bear charm and I had to special order it. He was most particular about the size. He showed me a chain he was wearing with two other small charms on it. He said he wanted the teddy bear to be the same size. He paid in advance, including the extra charge for a rush job."

"I'll need to take this, but I'll give you a receipt."

"But Mr. Morgan—"

"He won't be picking it up," Ohara said as he wrote the receipt. "He's dead."

"Oh, my," the jeweler said, "such a tragedy. You never know, do you?" Silently he put the charm back in the envelope and handed it over.

Ohara thanked him and left. He got into his car and headed

for the freeway into downtown Los Angeles and Little Tokyo. The doll shop, on a street of older shops, looked the same as it had when Grandfather Shimizu, master doll maker from Japan, had first opened it thirty years before. It was a permanent part of the Little Tokyo Ohara had know as a boy.

When he entered, he was as fascinated as he'd been the first time his parents had brought him there by the rows and rows of dolls in cases, and the proudly framed Japanese certificates attesting to Shimizu's rank and skill. He noted that two new certificates had been added, maintaining the family tradition through the generations.

When the more than middle-aged clerk heard his name, she at once recalled his family and politely offered tea. Ohara accepted, as was expected, and while she went to prepare it, he strolled around the small museum of dolls: samurai warriors of history, maidens of poetic legend, characters from the Noh plays, dramatic Lion Dancer dolls with startling white and red manes. There were several charming child dolls like the one he had with him.

When the tea came, he sipped and appreciated the delicate mountain blend. The clerk was Mrs. Okui, an elderly cousin of the Shimizu, who had more or less grown up in the business. Politely, she waited until he had finished his tea before she asked, "Why you come Shimizu, Ohara-san? Maybe buy nice doll?"

"No, I'm afraid I've come on other business." She looked alarmed, so he hastily added, "About this," taking the broken doll out of the manila envelope and laying it on the counter. "I came across it in the course of an investigation. I hoped you could tell me something about it. Is it one of yours?"

She took the little body into her hands, shaking her head sadly over the damage. She did not answer his question at once. "How this happen?"

"I don't know. I found it in a wastebasket."

"This not a Shimizu doll, Ohara-san. I think made by Shimizu pupil." Gently she parted the long black hair on the doll's head and, pointing to a tiny Japanese character scratched on the skull, nodded. "This one made by Yumi Kubota. She study Shimizu five years. Her mother bring her every week since she young child. Yumi have good hands. Sometimes we carry her dolls in the shop. Not so fine as Shimizu's work, but very good."

She went over to a shelf and brought back an exquisite Wisteria Dancer. The doll was dressed in a pale pink kimono; her head, with hair piled high in glossy waves, tipped daintily toward a spray of lavender silk blossoms held in an upraised hand. Even in its few painted lines, the face conveyed all the dreamy romanticism of a young girl in love.

Ohara studied the doll, lost in admiration. The girl Yumi had amazing talent. It seemed impossible that the person who had produced this small perfect thing could have anything to do with Morgan. "I'd like to buy it for my wife," he said at last. "It's beautiful."

Mrs. Okui was pleased. "Your wife will like, I know." Ohara watched as she wrapped the doll and case separately, in blue and white-patterned rice paper.

"Do you have Yumi Kubota's address?" he asked as she tied the packages with dark blue cord and added the traditional Japanese gift knot.

"I not know house, but Mrs. Kubota have small grocery store in Burbank, Kubota Grocery. There long time."

As Ohara paid for his purchase, she looked down at the broken doll. "And this little one?"

"I think I'll see if Miss Kubota can fix that. I want to talk to her."

He put the broken pieces back into the envelope. Mrs. Okui started to say something, but just then the shop door opened to admit a delivery boy with a precariously piled

[69]

load of boxes. Unable to see over the top of it, he almost crashed into a table of historical dolls. Sputtering protest, Mrs. Okui rushed over to him to prevent disaster.

Ohara had the information he needed. The Kubota Grocery in Burbank was undoubtedly one of the small business establishments on a street not too far from where Morgan's body had been found. He said a polite sayonara to Mrs. Okui as she cautiously shepherded the delivery boy to the rear of the store, picked up his packages and left. He would look up Yumi tomorrow.

It had been a successful afternoon, but uneasiness nagged at him as he started the long drive home. He should have heard something from Ted Washington. It worried him that Reilly's people in the field had not picked up a trace of him.

XI

For once, as he sat down to dinner, Ohara welcomed the shrill interruption of the telephone. It was Reilly. "Washington's flushed a new dealer playing it big. Could be Morgan's stash. He's going to make a buy tonight. We'll sweep them up. You want in?"

"You bet. Where and when?" Ohara wrote down the address and hung up the phone feeling better than he had in several hours.

The operation was set for nine-thirty, but by eight Ohara was cruising past the house where Washington was to make his buy. He felt uneasy. More so now that he'd seen the neighborhood. It was a street of drearily similar frame bungalows, their pride of being long since succumbed to peeling paint, brown stubble lawns and broken steps. He allowed himself only one drive-by, aware of the hostile stares that followed him from porches and steps, from kids playing in the street. It was the kind of place that had no welcome for strangers. The address Reilly had given him was in the middle of the block. A burned-out skeleton of a bungalow and its twin with a smeared "For Rent" sign tacked to the porch flanked it on either side. Light showed behind a torn window shade and, looking incongruous in its polished newness, a top-dollar motorcycle was parked beside the steps.

A Good Humor truck trailed Ohara down the street, but no customers stopped it. He wondered if the driver was one of Reilly's men. Turning off at the end of the street, he continued around the block. He pulled up at a fast-food stand on the corner from where he could see both approaches to the house. He bought a cold drink and nursed it as he settled down in the car to wait and watch the street.

A few minutes later a black Mustang with lowered front axle pulled up and parked in front of the house with the "For Rent" sign. After a moment two blacks got out and walked around to the back. They could be Reilly's people, but Ohara doubted it. Muscle-bound bloods like those were more likely protection for the dealer. Could be the Black Guerrilla Family had picked up Morgan's stuff after he was out of the running.

There were still almost forty minutes to wait. Suddenly, Ohara leaned forward and stared. Another car with three men in it had pulled up in front of the house. One of them got out and stood talking to the two in the car. There was no mistaking that tall, familiar figure. It was Washington, way ahead of time. Did Reilly know?

Washington was every inch the black dude on the make— tight jeans, boots, a yellow shirt open to the navel, a heavy gold chain gleaming against his bare chest. His face was shadowed by a wide-brimmed hat. He scratched at his nose in a junkie's itchy habit, then took out a cigarette and lit it. Ohara sensed he was stalling. As the car pulled away, he turned and, with a loose-limbed strut, began to walk up toward the house. He paused to admire the bike, then with a last look around, went up the steps and knocked at the door.

Ohara quickly got out of the car and walked along the opposite side of the street, his eyes on Washington. The door of the house opened briefly, then closed. He wondered where the two bloods were. It looked like a set-up.

He crossed the street and moved down the side of the house toward the rear yard. The back door was slightly ajar. Easing his gun into his hand, he pulled the door open and went into a dark and empty kitchen. Cautiously he pushed at a swing door that opened onto a short hall. Light streamed from a room ahead, where a voice grated, "All right, Mex. Up against the wall. You, too, big fella."

"You dirty bastard—you bring police—" A man's high-pitched shout was cut off by the sound of a blow.

Washington's voice, slurred and protesting, whined, "Man, these boys ain't police for sure. You the one set me up—"

Someone laughed. "You got it, big boy."

Ohara edged down the narrow hall to the doorway of the lighted room. He could just see Washington and a thin, long-haired Chicano spread-eagled against the wall. One of the blacks he'd seen earlier was pocketing a supply of balloons from the table while holding a gun on the victims. The other frisked their pockets, netting two large rolls of bills.

"Hey, listen, you guys," Washington tried, "I just wanted to make a buy. I don't want no trouble."

The big man who had pocketed the money answered him with a savage kick behind the knee, staggering him, then turned his attention to the Chicano. He spun the man around to face him. His partner with the gun watched, grinning.

"Flaco, you nothin' but a two-bit junkie that got lucky," he said. "Smokey's boys don't like no competition from you or nobody else. Got it?" His hand gripped Flaco's arm, twisting it up behind his back; he jerked upward until Flaco cried out in pain. "If you want to get out of this with no more than a busted ass, tell us where the stash is."

"What stash? I ain't got no more." His voice was breathy and thin with pain and fear.

The man with the gun came over and raked the barrel across Flaco's mouth, splitting his lip. Moaning, the Chicano tried to hold his torn mouth with his free hand.

"The stash you took from Morgan. Where is it?"

"Haven't got it," Flaco mumbled, trying to wipe away the blood. His face was pasty white and glistening with sweat.

There was no sound from the rest of the house, and the terrified, no-hope look on the Chicano's face told Ohara the man was playing it alone.

The black let go of Flaco's arm and shoved him back against the wall. "OK, we got other ways. How about a kneecap for a start? Which one will it be?"

Flaco touched his lips painfully with his tongue, but did not answer.

The blacks exchanged a look, then the man with the gun pointed it at the victim's right knee. His finger slowly began to close on the trigger.

Ohara spun around the side of the door, crouched and aimed. "Police! Freeze!"

The gunman turned, startled, jerking his trigger finger so that the shot went over Ohara's head into the door frame. Ohara's bullet went into the man's thigh. He crumpled with a scream, dropping his gun as he grabbed at his leg.

The second man reached for his gun, but Washington's long leg swung out in a roundhouse kick that swept it out of his hand; fingers like iron spikes plunged between the intruder's ribs and a quick chop to the neck dropped him.

Flaco, standing motionless, saw Ohara bend to pick up the gun near his feet. Washington was stooping for the second gun when he caught the flash of Flaco's hand pulling a knife strapped to his calf. "Look out, Sam!"

Alerted, Ohara turned so that he took the knife thrust in his arm. The force of it threw him backward and Flaco pushed past him out the door. Washington bent over Ohara, "You OK?"

Ohara nodded. "Get him!"

Washington ran for the door. Flaco, one arm hanging at his side, was trying to turn the motorcycle toward the street. Washington leaped down the steps, launched himself at

Flaco, and they went down in a heap. Three men, Reilly in the lead, ran up the narrow walk, pulled the struggling bodies apart and jerked them to their feet.

"Ohara's hurt," Washington said and led the way inside to the back room where Ohara, his back against the wall, covered the two blacks with his gun. Blood dripped from the arm hanging at his side.

"What the hell went down here?" Reilly muttered, then sent a man to call for an ambulance. Washington took Ohara's gun. "We got him!"

"Forget these jokers." Reilly came over to Ohara. "There's an ambulance on the way."

Ohara shook his head, "No ambulance. Just needs a tight bandage."

"Got a handkerchief?" Washington asked.

"Left pocket," Ohara replied. Reilly was already offering his. With the two, Washington made a pressure pad and tied it firmly.

"Thanks, partner." Ohara smiled. "I owe you."

"No sweat." Washington cut it short, but he liked the sound of that "partner." He was no longer the new boy.

Reilly surveyed the two on the floor. The man Washington had dropped was still out cold. The one who'd been shot groaned miserably. "Ambulance on the way, fella," Reilly said. "You'll live."

He turned back to Washington and Ohara, then jerked his head toward Flaco, standing sullenly against the wall, his mouth bloody and swollen.

"He's the dealer I was meeting," Washington answered. "The other two are from Smokey's crowd. They jumped us."

"You changed the time, Washington. Why didn't you check in?"

"Sorry about that, but Flaco decided to play it cagey. Set

the time I told you, then sent two guys to pick me up early and bring me over here. They didn't even give me a chance to go to the can."

Reilly looked at Ohara. "How come you were here?"

"I was wondering that, too." Washington grinned. "You sure saved my ass."

Ohara shrugged, then wished he hadn't. "After you called Reilly, I got itchy. I wanted to see the setup, so I came early for a quick drive past and parked down the street to wait for you. I saw those two go into the vacant house next door. In a few minutes Washington arrived ahead of schedule with an escort. Thought I'd better check it out."

"That's what I call backup, partner."

Ohara smiled and continued. "When I got in the house, Smokey's boys had them both against the wall. They wanted to trade Flaco a kneecap for the stash. So I broke up the action. Washington did the rest."

Reilly looked at the mayhem on the floor. "You boys play rough. Which one got you, Sam?"

Ohara nodded at Flaco. "He did."

Washington glared at the Chicano. "Some gratitude. He owes Ohara his life; Smokey's boys would have made dog meat out of him."

"I don't owe nobody nothin', you bloody pig." Flaco snarled, "I'd have done them myself…"

"That's enough," Reilly interrupted. He looked at the man guarding Flaco. "Read him his rights."

When this had been done, he said, "This your house Flaco?"

"No. My mama's. I got every right here. She's away."

Reilly held up a document. "This says we can take the place apart to find the stash. Your mama won't like that. So why don't you just hand it over?"

Flaco sneered, as well as he could with his battered mouth. "You wastin' your time. Nothin' to find."

"Smokey's boys know different. So do we."

"I decided I want a lawyer and a doc. That's my rights."

Reilly nodded. "OK, Flaco, first the hospital, then you can call a lawyer. You might need him; looks like somebody might have killed Morgan for that stash."

Defiance went out of Flaco and fear took its place. "I didn' kill nobody. Don' know no Morgan."

"Where'd these balloons come from?" Reilly held up the balloons Flaco's assailant had pocketed.

"I was pushin' for a pal." Flaco stared at the skeptical faces surrounding him and his shoulders slumped. "So you get me for pushin', big deal."

The ambulance arrived and Reilly's man nudged Flaco toward the door. He went, eyes on the ground, muttering to himself. Ohara was close enough behind to hear the loser's litany, "Same shit luck all my whole fuckin' life…never nothin' but shit…" A string of pain-relieving obscenities followed. They were the only form of protest Flaco knew; he had long ago forgotten how to cry.

XII

FLACO felt as if the pale green walls of the interrogation room were closing in on him. Painfully he puffed on the cigarette he'd been given. The stitches in his lip hurt like hell and his shoulder ached, but he'd toughed it out. Never let the cops see you were afraid, or they'd pull you down. That was a credo he lived by. He had to think up a deal they'd buy, but it was hard to keep his head straight with the cold gut-fear eating him.

The gray-haired narc and the Jap cop, with his arm bandaged, were facing him across the table along with the public defender lawyer they'd got him. The black dude who'd trapped him was leaning against the wall, and a cop with a notebook sat in the corner. They were all looking at him. It made him feel like a bug in a bottle. He took another painful drag on the cigarette and scratched his itchy nose.

He needed a fix, needed it bad, and real soon. If it weren't for that he'd let them suck their thumbs and wait. Guess he'd have to tell them what they wanted to hear so they'd get him a shot of meth or something. Course, that was only a penny when he needed a buck, but it was better than nothing. He tried to control a creeping nausea so he could think. It was worse than usual since he'd been living it up on Morgan's stuff. Out of habit he rolled the cigarette across his lips and almost cried out in pain. Smokey's boys catching up with him was an angle he hadn't figured.

He didn't have much to bargain with. Since they'd found the stash behind the loose brick in the fireplace, the cops held the high cards. It hadn't needed any college kid public defender to point that out. Well, let the guy sit there and take notes; he'd make his own deal.

"OK, Flaco, you know what we've got on you, so quit stalling and tell us about Morgan." The gray-haired narc looked like somebody's good old dad, but he was a hard-nosed bastard just the same.

Flaco took his time, then said, "What's in it for me?"

"You'll look better in court."

"That so?" Flaco shot the question at the lawyer, who shrugged, then nodded agreement.

"How much better?" Flaco sniffed and scraped at his nose.

"For openers, you might convince us you didn't kill Morgan."

"Jeez, how many times I got to tell you. I didn' kill nobody."

"You're pretty quick with a knife." Reilly glanced over at Ohara, then continued. "You wouldn't be the first to commit murder for a bag of heroin like Morgan had."

Flaco licked his lips and winced, wishing he had time to think. Why didn't the goddamn lawyer object or something? He shivered, thinking about finding the bag. For a little while he'd had it all...a permanent high, money, women, an insurance policy against anyone pushing him around again. Now the fucking bag could finish him.

Reilly hammered on. "Must have been easy shaking down his apartment when you knew he wouldn't be walking in on you."

Flaco sensed the danger even without the lawyer's finally starting to object. He pulled himself together. "Yeah, sure, I knew he was dead...from the papers. Why pick on me? Go find the guy Morgan made the deal with." In the silence that followed, he knew he'd got them. With satisfaction he ground out his cigarette stub in the ashtray in front of him.

Ohara took up the questioning. "Tell us about Morgan from the beginning."

Flaco flicked his eyes over at him, then away. He'd have to watch out with the Jap cop, he'd be out to nail him sure for cutting his arm up. "Smokey gave me what I needed personal," he said, "but coupla times I came up short on the bread and he tol' me to get lost. A pal put me on to Morgan, said he was a new dealer with big connections, and was musclin' in on Smokey. I figured he might give a guy a break. Soon as I got some new bread I set up a meet."

"Where?" Reilly cut in.

"Hokey's Place in Pacoima."

"Near the community college," Ohara said.

"Yeah, Morgan worked that place; Smokey didn' have the class." Flaco was enjoying his new importance.

"Go on," Ohara prompted.

"Morgan was sittin' at one of the tables when I got there. I passed him the dough and he handed back a bag of fries with the balloons inside. Neat, huh? The guy was creepy but he was cool."

"What do you mean, creepy?" Ohara thought the description didn't fit the Morgan image.

Flaco shrugged. "He wore these brown sunglasses, and I mean all the time, so you couldn' see his eyes. Sorta trademark. Even doin' business he treated you like you was dirt or somethin'. Smokey always was a joker except when he was sore. I could dig him. Then there was the way Morgan acted with the chick..."

"Did he have a girl with him?" Ohara asked.

"No. This was a kid who just walked by. She works in the Jap grocery next to Hokey's."

Ohara's face showed no change but this was the first link to the broken Japanese doll in Morgan's wastebasket. "Did she know Morgan?"

"You kiddin'? Yumi wouldn' know a creep like Morgan. She was just passin' by on her way home, but she sure turned him on. He even stopped talkin' to stare at her. She's a looker and you could tell he was strippin' her down. His face got sort of funny and he watched her all the way down the block. Bad scene!"

"You said her name was Yumi, you know her?"

"Yeah, she's a neighborhood kid. Everybody knows Yumi."

Ohara wanted more; he lit a cigarette and handed it to Flaco. "Looks like she was Morgan's type."

"I tol' you she was a real doll. But I grew up with her, see, and in her head she's just a little kid. I wised Morgan up about that, how she don' talk or hear, and how the neighborhood guys look out for her like she's a mascot sorta."

"What happened then?"

"Nothin'. He just sorta smiled and said he wasn't interested in Japs anyway. Then he tol' me to move it. Last I see of him he was sittin' there playin' with those goddamn kid charms he wore on a gold chain."

"Charms? You mean he wore more than one?" To Flaco's surprise, Washington came away from the wall to stand next to Ohara.

Flaco took his time. He liked making the black dude wait. "Yeah," he said at last, "he had two."

"Hold it a minute, Flaco." Ohara stood up and said to the others, "There's something in my office I'd like Flaco to look at. I'll go get it."

In a few minutes he was back with a glassine envelope. He took out the small bicycle charm it contained and held it so Flaco could see it. "Is this one of the charms?"

"Could be. I kinda remember one was a bicycle, not sure about the other. Can you dig that? A guy like Morgan wearing kiddy charms!"

There was a silence as Ohara put the charm away, then Flaco made his play. "I don' feel so good. If I don' get a shot or somethin' soon, I'm gonna split in two. I'm hurtin' too much to talk any more." He shuddered, then hugged his arms against his stomach and began to rock back and forth on his chair.

Washington stared down at him. "You don't get anything until we're finished here. How long it takes is up to you."

Flaco hunched his body. "Jeez, what else?"

The lawyer spoke up. "My client needs attention."

Flaco eyed him with contempt. "About time you opened your mouth."

Reilly took charge, pleasant but determined. "Your client has been attended by a doctor, counselor. He was certified as well enough to be questioned. If he needs further care he'll get it when we're finished."

The lawyer sighed and sat back.

"When did you see Morgan next?" Reilly continued the questioning.

"Next night, at the St. Jude's Carnival."

"Did you talk to him?"

"Naw, I saw him meet this big guy...looked like he knew him from someplace."

"Ever seen him before?"

Flaco shook his head. "Nope, but I figure that kinda info was worth somethin' to the right people. I squeezed up behind 'em so's I could hear, but they got in the big wheel and went round a few times to do their talkin'. Then the big dude splits and I follow Morgan." He leaned back, exhausted. "Hey, you gotta give me a drink."

"Here." Reilly set a pitcher of water and glass in front of him. Looking disgusted, Flaco made them wait while he poured himself a drink. "What happened then?" Reilly persisted.

Flaco thought a minute then went on. "Morgan did a funny

thing. On the way out he spots Yumi standin' at the baseball pitch and he stops dead. She had a friend with her, guy named Kenji."

"Who's Kenji?" Ohara asked.

"Neighborhood guy. He lives with old lady Kubota and Yumi."

"What's the rest of his name?"

"Kimura, Kenji Kimura."

"Get back to Morgan." Reilly was growing impatient.

Flaco stared at him and took another long drink of water, then he turned back to Ohara. "The baseball pitch had some pink teddy bears for prizes and Yumi put on a big act so's Kenji should win her one. He buys some balls and gives it a try, but he ain't gettin' no place. Then Morgan goes over, buys in, zings six good ones and wins a teddy bear. When he gets it, he hands it to Yumi and walks off. You know, it doesn't figure. That guy don' give nothin' to nobody. Why'd he do it?" Nobody answered so he went on. "Anyway, after that he just went home. I followed him on my bike."

Ohara thought about the teddy bear charm that was Morgan's last purchase and left it to Reilly to ferret out Flaco's whereabouts on the day Morgan was killed. The Chicano had an alibi of sorts by claiming that he and a buddy had shared a lucky numbers ticket and got stoned together for two days.

"What's his name?" Reilly squeezed for the last drop.

"Chino...just Chino." Flaco was beginning to twitch. His nose seemed worse; he couldn't keep his hands off it.

"Where can we find Chino?"

"Don' know. He sleeps around."

"You better come up with something, man." Washington leaned over him and spelled it out. "He's your alibi for Morgan's murder."

Fear was back in Flaco's face; his eyes mutely questioned the lawyer.

"He's right. Chino's your witness. You're going to need him."

"Chino—" Flaco swallowed, looking miserable. "He moves around like, but sometimes he works at Hokey's." When Reilly said they'd find him, Flaco still didn't look too happy.

That about wound it up, and Ohara and Washington headed back to their office. "His alibi's weak, Sam. I think we could break it, then everything else would fit."

"Yes," Ohara agreed, "but there's another angle. I'm expecting some information from the King City police. It could change a lot of things." With a wince of pain, he sat down and brought Washington up to date on what he'd been doing.

As he finished, a uniformed officer brought in a large manila envelope, special delivery from King City. Eagerly Ohara opened it. It contained the records of the King City rape-murder case in which Morgan had been questioned and released.

Washington scanned the closely typed pages over Ohara's shoulder. "Poor little kid," he said, his fists involuntarily bunching.

Ohara felt his stomach tighten as he took from his pocket the small gold bicycle charm found on Morgan's body. He held it so his partner could see the date. "September 4," Washington said softly, "and according to the record, the King City victim was discovered on September 6."

"Yes," Ohara said, then read from the file before them. "The child's bicycle was found close to the scene of the murder."

XIII

OHARA took out Morgan's last purchase, the teddy bear charm, and laid it beside the tiny gold bicycle.

"I've heard of all kinds of rapist souvenirs," Washington said, "from locks of hair to shoes in the closet, but if these were Morgan's souvenirs I have to admit he was different." He separated the two small charms. "The date on the bicycle charm and the King City murder are consistent. But the only event that matches up with the date on the teddy bear is Morgan's death."

"And," Ohara added, "the fact that Morgan was seen to give Yumi Kubota a teddy bear."

"You think she was next on the list?"

"Undoubtedly."

"But there's been no recent rape-murder."

"True, the log of that date shows nothing, Ted, but there are other possibilities."

"You mean like he might have been killed before he could pull it off."

"That's one. Maybe he stopped short of murder this time. Let's check the rape reports." Ohara picked up the phone and asked for Records. After a few minutes he put it down again, frowning. "Records has no rape report for that date either. Of course, many go unreported."

"Looks like we're back to square one again."

"Maybe not," Ohara said thoughtfully. "Let's say Yumi was the victim. She may have been too afraid to even speak about the rape to anyone. Some Japanese girls are like that—" Ohara stopped short. "We're forgetting something else, Ted. Flaco said she was deaf and dumb."

"Her mother could have reported it."

"You're underestimating Japanese reticence. Some of the older people still believe a private disgrace is better than a public one."

His expression grim, Washington had to agree. "A rape investigation is pretty public."

"Suppose," Ohara extended his line of thinking, "a relative, or say a friend, walked in on Morgan while he was at it, and killed him in trying to save the girl."

"What about the boy she was with at the carnival, Kenji something?"

"Yes, he's a possible, but we need to know more about him. Could he take a guy like Morgan? There's another angle, too. Flaco told Morgan that 'the guys would take care of anybody that messed with Yumi.'"

"If they had, Morgan wouldn't have died with all his parts on him."

"We'd better check Kenji out first, Ted. Flaco might give us a line on him. See if you can find out where the boy was the day Morgan was killed."

"Anything else?"

"Not yet. I'll go see the girl or her mother. It'll be tricky since we don't have much of a handle. But I have got one thing." He reached into his desk drawer and took out the broken doll. "This lady may get me on first base."

"This is the doll you found in Morgan's place, right?" Washington picked up the head and ran his finger over the long black hair. "Feels real." Carefully he fitted the head to the small body. "Pretty. Wonder why the bastard snapped the neck in two."

"Dress rehearsal, I would guess," Ohara answered, his face hard. "I wish we could track down that other charm. It would strengthen our case."

Washington brightened. "The computer could give us any

unsolved rape-killings in the state before 1976 when Morgan was sent up. I'll give it a try."

"That's a good angle." Ohara stood up, cradling his injured arm. "Also, see if there's anything new on Morgan's car."

"Will you be coming back to the office later?"

"No. I don't know how long it'll take to see the girl and her mother. After I do, I think I'll go home. Peggy was pretty well shaken up about last night. She'll feel better if she can have me to fuss over for a while."

"So will you, I bet. Why don't you just go home, Sam? I'll see the women for you."

"Thanks, but I think speaking Japanese may come in handy with them. See you in the morning."

Half an hour later Ohara parked across the street from the Kubota Grocery. He sat behind the wheel a few minutes thinking about the sometimes unbalanced scales of justice. Everything pointed to Morgan being the brutal rapist-murderer of at least one young girl. Ohara felt he was close to proving that Morgan had tried again. He found it ironic that he must do his best to find out who had killed the killer.

For the sake of those whose lives he was going to invade, he wished it had been simple self-defense, but it hadn't. Morgan's head had been deliberately pulled back and the knife thrust through the base of the throat. He sensed the killing had been done in the primitive compulsions of hate and vengeance. It was the first shadowy line in the profile of Morgan's unknown killer. With a sigh he got out of the car and walked across the street. Like it or not, he had a job to do.

The grocery was a small one, the last of a dying breed. It was Japanese from the Kanji-English sign to the fat, ceramic cat with its left paw raised in the corner of the window. He hadn't seen a *maneki-neko*, a beckoning cat, for quite a while. Old-fashioned storekeepers thought them as essential as the cash register, since they were reputed to invite customers in and bring prosperity.

It looked as if this one was on the job. The store had two customers when he entered. He strolled over to the vegetable bins, admiring the way they'd been arranged with an instinctive eye for color appeal. A teenage boy was sprinkling them with water.

As Ohara waited for the store to clear, he pretended to search the grocery shelves. Actually he was glad of the short wait. It gave him a chance to study the woman behind the counter. The white butcher's apron she wore made her small heavyset body look almost square. The broad planes of her face were emphasized by the way her gray hair was drawn to the top of her head in an old-fashioned knot held in place by two long black lacquer hairpins, old-style Japanese *kanzashi*. From his boyhood, Ohara remembered an aunt who'd worn them just that way. She'd been a practical, nononsense woman. He surmised that Mrs. Kubota was much the same.

She was now waiting on the last customer, an elderly woman whose shrill Japanese carried all over the store. She had a complaint and made the most of it. "Kubota-san, why you leave me standing knocking at your door last Thursday? You know Thursday is my appointment time, right at six o'clock. There I was, but no one let me in."

She stopped to catch her breath, holding up a wrinkled hand to forestall interruption; she had more to get off her chest. "You know very well that only the silver needles help my poor back. You don't have time? No matter, Yumi can do. She gave me a good treatment before."

"So sorry, *Okusan*." Mrs. Kubota sweetened her apology with several short bows. "Last Thursday we had an emergency at the store. I could not get home for your treatment.

You don't have a telephone so I could not call. Please forgive. Next Thursday, you come and I give treatment for free."

"For free? I will come." The old lady allowed herself to be mollified. "Next Thursday, then. I come. Six o'clock sharp. You will be there please, Kubota-san." She took out a worn brocade purse and painstakingly counted out the coins for her can of cat food. Ohara watched Mrs. Kubota tuck a package of noodles into the bag as well. Without comment the old lady picked up her purchase and left.

"Sayonara, *Okusan. Ja mata*." Mrs. Kubota's wide smile ushered the old lady out the door, then faded as her square body slumped against the counter. It was only when Ohara began to walk toward her that she noticed him. "*Hai*, you want something?"

Hoping to put her at ease, Ohara used Japanese. "I couldn't help overhearing. Do you do acupuncture?"

A shadow crossed the woman's face. For a moment she just stared at him, her eyes anxious, then she said in her own language, "My husband used to do acupuncture. He had a license and he taught me. Sometime I still do it for old patients."

"I understand," Ohara smiled reassuringly. "Actually, I came about something else." He held out his ID. For a moment she seemed to stop breathing, then she called over to the boy. "Shig, please to sweep front sidewalk."

"OK," the boy mumbled. Mrs. Kubota turned her attention back to Ohara.

"Nothing is wrong here for the police. Why do you come?"

He took the doll out of a large mailing envelope. Mrs. Kubota stared at it, her stolid expression revealing nothing. "I came across this in an investigation. Shimizu's doll shop said that your daughter, Yumi, had made it. I'd like to ask some questions about it."

Shig, his ears tuned, walked as slowly as possible past them and out the door, the pushbroom like a rifle across his shoulder. Ohara felt the woman's tension lessen. "Yes, my daughter, Yumi, made it. I sell them in the shop." She pointed behind her to two other dolls on a shelf behind the counter.

"Your daughter is a fine artist," Ohara said, meaning it. He laid the pieces of the broken doll on the counter. "Do you remember to whom you sold it?"

"No, I don't remember," she said, setting her lips in a tight stubborn line.

Ohara reached into his pocket and took out the ID picture of Morgan. "Was it this man?" He laid the picture on the counter beside the doll. She looked at it but said nothing.

"We found the doll in his apartment, after he was killed."

Her left hand went suddenly to her heart, then, as if aware that Ohara had noticed, she moved it jerkily to smooth her hair. Still she said nothing.

Ohara waited as she nervously adjusted one of the black lacquer *kanzashi*, revealing a quarter inch of silver metal. The *kanzashi* he remembered from his youth had not been made like that. "Do you recognize this man as the one who bought the doll?" he repeated.

She sighed. "Yes, maybe he was the one who bought it."

"He was found stabbed to death not far from here," Ohara went on, watching her face. It might have been a Kabuki mask for all the reaction it showed.

"That is a bad thing. I think I saw it in paper, now that you say it happened near here. He was an American *yakusa*, I think." She used the Japanese term for gangster or mafioso, a word seldom spoken aloud in Japan.

"Why do you say that?" Ohara asked.

"I just think—" she began and stopped.

Ohara became conscious of movement behind him. Mrs.

[92]

Kubota's eyes widened in alarm and both her hands came down on the counter across Morgan's picture. He turned quickly and his movement threw him against a girl standing just behind him. "*Sumimasen...*" he began to apologize.

The girl shook her head smiling, then she put her hands on her knees and bowed an apology in return. It was an old-fashioned custom, totally unexpected from a slim young woman in white slacks and tee-shirt.

Behind him Mrs. Kubota was saying, "Excuse please, Ohara-san. My daughter, Yumi, is careless; she should not have come here."

"It's all right." He smiled at Yumi. "It was my fault. I hope I didn't—"

He was stopped by Yumi's soft fingers against his lips. Then she put her hands over her own ears, then across her lips, all the time shaking her head in negation. He'd forgotten she couldn't speak or hear. The simple explanation of her handicap touched him. She had shown no embarrassment in her childlike movements.

It was difficult to believe that the mind behind those intelligent dark eyes was retarded. Yet there was an innocence in her expression that went only with the very young. She'd made herself understood very well; better than he could have under the circumstances. Her modern clothes seemed an anachronism. With her delicate, aristocratic features, she reminded him of the elegant geishas Utamaro had made famous in his prized woodblock prints. He imagined her in a kimono with her heavy schoolgirl braid of hair pulled high with coral combs, a model for one of the historic dolls she made.

Mrs. Kubota came from behind the counter. "*Gomen nasai,*" she muttered, then going over to the girl, she shook her by the shoulders and pointed toward the back room. As rebellion filled Yumi's eyes, she looked like any eight-year-old resenting discipline. Her red lips pouted. Pushing her mother's hands away she moved toward Ohara.

As she did so she saw the broken doll on the counter. The change in her was dramatic. She snatched up the little body, making soft mewing sounds of distress as her fingers explored the damage. A tear slid down her cheek.

Ohara put out his hand. "I'm sorry," he began, again forgetting her deafness. She looked up at him and her eyes, wide, staring, filled with violent anger, shocked him. Still holding the doll, she beat against his chest with her fists until he captured her hands and forced them to be still. He held her eyes with his own, willing her to be calm. Gradually her body relaxed against him. He took the doll from her and pointing to it and then to himself, he shook his head no. She studied his face for a moment, then took the doll back and carefully fitted the head onto the broken neck. She looked at him to be sure he understood. She would fix it.

Ohara smiled back and nodded, and her happy smile flashed, bathing him in approval.

Mrs. Kubota once more took Yumi by the shoulders and began to guide her toward the back room. "My daughter is not well now. She must go home."

Ohara stood staring after them, aware but not caring that some of his questions were still unanswered. So far he had always managed to keep himself personally detached from the people he met in the course of his job, but even in this brief time he knew he was caught up with Yumi—contradictory, half little girl, half woman, and completely fascinating.

As the two women reached the door, Yumi turned back to smile and wave at him with the happy abandon of a child. He realized that he would have been disappointed if she hadn't, and waved back, amused at his own lighthearted reaction.

As he turned back to the counter he saw the corner of Roy Morgan's picture jutting from beneath a carton of Hershey bars where Mrs. Kubota had hidden it. He pulled it out and shoved it into his pocket, the thought of Yumi in Morgan's hands making him sick with anger. Mrs. Kubota's fear that Yumi might see the picture told its own story. He, too, now feared what might happen when he showed it to Yumi, as he must. Any pleasure at the thought of seeing her again was gone.

As he left the store, he almost fell over Shig, whose sweeping had apparently been confined to the area nearest the door. The boy stopped working at once. "You a cop, mister?"

"Yes," Ohara said, and waited.

"Bet you're here about the guy that was murdered down the street. I saw him, you know. He was in our store. Boy, what a build." Unconsciously Shig's narrow shoulders straightened.

"Did you wait on him?" This was unexpected pay dirt.

"No, the old lady—I mean, Mrs. Kubota did. She sold him one of Yumi's dolls. Hey, was he really burned by the Mafia?"

"We can't say as yet, Shig." Not wanting to turn the boy off, he went on. "But if you know anything about him, it would help us to find out."

"No, I don't know nothing." Shig looked deflated.

About to turn away, Ohara remembered something. "I understand you had an emergency at the store a week ago… Thursday, wasn't it? What happened?"

Shig frowned. "We didn't have no emergency. I know, because Thursdays I work from five to nine so Mrs. Kubota can go home by six. She didn't say anything when I came on and nothing happened afterward."

Ohara thanked Shig and walked across to his car, mentally fitting the new puzzle pieces into place: Mrs. Kubota was afraid...last Thursday at the crucial time she failed to keep a regular appointment...she'd hidden Morgan's picture from Yumi...and the *kanzashi* in her hair were not the usual lacquered wood, but had strong metal shanks that could have pierced a man's throat. Lastly, and with reluctance, he acknowledged the blind unreasoning rage that had flashed in Yumi's eyes and disappeared again without a trace. If she'd been violated, like the broken doll, for her to strike back, to kill, would have been as natural as breathing.

XIV

Oʜᴀʀᴀ edged his car out from behind a small gray Honda that had not been there when he'd arrived. He drove mechanically, his mind on the Kubotas and the fact that mother and daughter were trained in acupuncture. They had the knowledge and skill to kill Morgan as he had been killed, but the scenario didn't fit, at least not without something more to go on.

He cut off further speculation and concentrated on the rush hour traffic. As he glanced into the driving mirror before making a lane change, he noticed a gray Honda behind him. When he turned onto the freeway to Burbank, the car followed. It looked like the one that had been parked at the Kubota Grocery. On a hunch, he moved quickly into the far left lane just before the freeway split; the Honda cut across too. His suspicion became a probability. He wondered if the Honda would follow him down the Burbank off-ramp.

He left it to the last minute to cross into the ramp lane, but when he stopped for the street traffic light, the Honda was one car back. Ohara entered Burbank Boulevard and picked up speed. Since the brown Chevy now behind him was a tailgater, the Honda was temporarily blocked. He hit the next signal on the yellow and turned right, leaving the Chevy and the Honda stuck at the light. Turning left into an alley concealed by a line of parked cars, he raced past two intersections and pulled into the parking lot of a neighborhood theater where he could watch the boulevard. In a few minutes he saw the Honda drive past, slowing down at the intersection for a look-see. The driver was Leo Krepp, the reporter. There was no mistaking that stringy red hair. As

Ohara pulled out of the parking lot to follow the follower, he noticed a black Mercedes closing in behind the smaller car. He fell in behind and trailed the two cars for a few blocks, noticing that the Mercedes slowed when the Honda slowed and made no attempt to pass.

Glad that he was driving his official car, Ohara picked up the mike and called in. "Ohara in Charley Fifty-seven. I'm checking out a tail job...black Mercedes seventy-eight or seventy-nine, X Ray Young Sam four five three."

In seconds he had a reply. "Ohara, Charley Fifty-seven. Mercedes X Ray Young Sam four five three...no wants... owner, Rafael Montero, 1372 Brentwood Drive."

"Ten four," Ohara answered and hung up the mike. Considering Krepp's pointed innuendos about Lucky Montero in his last article, the newsman could be in trouble. He pulled up abreast of the Mercedes to take a look. There were two men in the front seat with gang soldier written all over them. The driver had a noticeable harelip, which his heavy mustache failed to conceal. The men were absorbed in watching the progress of the Honda. Ohara picked up the mike again. "Ohara, Charley Fifty-seven. Black Mercedes X Ray Young Sam four five three driving north on 1300 block Burbank Boulevard...two Adam Henry's following gray Honda. Request backup to intercept, check licenses."

Even as the call was acknowledged, he switched on his red light and siren, passed the Mercedes, then pulled up opposite Krepp and waved him over to the curb. The Mercedes continued slowly past them and stopped at the end of the block. He'd try to keep Krepp talking until the patrol car could arrive, then get him out of there.

As Ohara got out of his car and went over to the Honda, Krepp stuck his head out of the window, aflame with indignation. "What'd you pull me over for, Ohara?"

Ignoring the belligerence, Ohara managed a smile. "You've

[98]

been going to a lot of trouble to follow me around. I assumed you wanted to talk to me, so talk."

"Last time you brushed me off. What's the matter? Don't you like what you're reading in the paper? I'm getting my own facts now. Who needs you!"

Ohara kept his temper, hoping the patrol car would soon arrive. "Sorry you feel that way, Krepp. You'll get the same story as the rest of the press when there's one to tell. And it'll be facts, not guesses. Don't try to force my hand or you'll regret it."

"Bullshit!" Krepp sounded macho tough, but Ohara's expression made him cautious enough to draw his head back within the safety of the car.

"There's no bullshit about this, Krepp. You were being followed by two hard types in a black Mercedes. They looked like a couple of Nuestra Familia soldiers. Maybe they didn't like what you wrote about them. They're parked at the end of the next block. I pulled you over to tell you. Look for yourself—" Ohara stopped abruptly. He'd been so absorbed with Krepp, the Mercedes had driven off and he hadn't noticed. "They've gone," he said.

"Yeah, sure." Krepp laughed. "The only black Mercedes was the one you dreamed up when I started talking harassment. Your buddies might believe you, but my readers won't."

Ohara leaned close, his black eyes hard. "If I ever did decide to lean on you, mister, I'd do a hell of a lot more than pull you over. Believe me, there was a Mercedes with two soldier types right on your tail. You'd have seen them if you hadn't been so busy chasing me."

"Can I go now?" Krepp cut in, his tone surly.

Ohara shrugged and started back to his car. A patrol car passed them, searching for the Mercedes. "Talk about pie in the face," Ohara muttered as the Honda U-turned and headed back toward the freeway. He drove to where the patrol car was parked two blocks down and made his apologies.

From an alley on the other side of the street the Mercedes merged in the traffic heading for the freeway. Krepp was stopped by the light, but he didn't notice the black automobile two cars behind him.

The next morning Leo Krepp was in the news, though not under his own byline. The report stated that Krepp, apparently the victim of a mugging, had been found in a downtown Los Angeles alley. The freelance reporter who had been doing a series of articles on alleged gang-related murders had been taken to the hospital and was still unconscious.

XV

WHEN Ohara heard the news about Krepp, he called Eddie Baker and told him about the black Mercedes belonging to Montero's brother that had been following the reporter. Baker jumped on it.

"Thanks, Ohara. That gives us something to go on. Describe the soldiers."

Despite the few seconds he'd observed them, Ohara came up with a fairly accurate description. When he mentioned the driver's harelip, Baker was jubilant. "I know him. Harelip was one of the friends who alibied Lucky Montero on the Lopez hit. He hangs out in my turf, so I'm pretty sure I can put my hands on him. Maybe I can get something bigger than a mugging out of this. Think Krepp will identify?"

"Depends on how much they put the fear of Nuestra Familia into him. Then again, he might think he's got the story of a lifetime and run with it."

Washington came in as Ohara was talking to Baker. "See you got the word on Krepp," he said when Ohara put down the phone. "What happened with the Kubotas?"

Ohara told him and asked what he had turned up on Kenji Kimura.

"He's lived with the Kubotas ever since his parents died in an accident when he was a kid. Flaco said they'd been close pals before he left the neighborhood. The two kids used to look after Yumi, and between them they'd clean up on anybody who tried to push her around."

Ohara was quiet as the mental kaleidoscope changed again. "Anything else?"

"Yes." Washington paused significantly, then went on. "Kenji works in an upholstery shop during the day. The owner's a Caucasian named Konecko. Kenji also goes to city college classes every Monday, Wednesday and Friday. He's studying pre-med."

"No classes on Thursday?"

"No, I checked."

"Maybe that was Morgan's bad luck. Let's go see Kenji."

Konecko's upholstery shop was in a storefront building on Burbank Boulevard. Its small front room became an office only by courtesy of the desk, two chairs and a telephone that sat with businesslike neatness among numerous fabric display books, an expertly upholstered love seat, and a long counter where a woman was trying sample fabrics against a worn-out couch cushion. Rainbow-hued Indian brocades hung from the ceiling in graceful folds. A short gray-haired man looked over at them from the counter. "I'll be with you in a few minutes."

When he had finished with the woman he came over to them. "What can I do for you?"

"We'd like to speak to Mr. Konecko." Ohara showed him his ID.

"I'm Konecko," the man said, frowning. "What do you want with me?"

"Not you, Mr. Konecko. We're looking for Kenji Kimura. I believe he works for you."

"Kenji?" Konecko looked astounded and his voice rose slightly. "Yes, he works for me. He's one of my best men."

"We'd like to talk to him."

"He's not in trouble, is he?" There was real concern in Konecko's voice.

"We're just making a routine check," Ohara soothed.

"Oh—it's about that car accident, isn't it?" Konecko said. "Kenji was badly banged up when he came to work on Friday."

"The accident was on Thursday?" Washington asked.

"Yes, Thursday night. Kenji's face looked like it had been beaten with a club. Couldn't have been his fault. He's very careful. You know, one time—"

Ohara stopped the flow. "May we see him, please?"

"Of course. The workroom is back here." Konecko led the way behind a partition through a narrow archway. "Kenji," he called, "the police are here about the accident."

Inwardly, Ohara groaned, and he looked at Washington, who shared his dismay. A man stuffing a cushion looked up. "Kenji just left, Mr. Konecko. Said he wasn't feeling well."

It was about what Ohara had expected, but Mr. Konecko went over to a table where an armchair stood upended, partially sewn welting hanging from the bottom. "That's not like him. He never leaves his work like this."

Behind him, Ohara and Washington stared at the tools laid out on the table with the precision of a fine craftsman. Washington picked up one of the long curved needles. "Must take a lot of strength to push one of these through all that padding."

"Yes, it does," Konecko agreed. "Kenji has very strong hands."

They thanked Konecko and left. "Want me to put out an APB?" Washington asked.

Ohara shook his head. "We won't have any trouble finding him."

"Even when we do, Sam, we've damn little to go on. If he keeps his mouth shut and nobody else opens theirs, he'll have it made."

"It's happened before," Ohara agreed as they walked toward

the car. "Trouble is, the one person I think knows what happened can't talk. Maybe we could—"

A man's voice interrupted. "Excuse me. You wanted to see me? I'm Kenji Kimura."

Surprised, they looked at the young Japanese-American. "Thought you went home sick," Washington said as Kenji looked nervously from one to the other.

"I wasn't feeling too good, so I stepped out for a breath of air. Mr. Konecko just told me you wanted to see me...about the car accident."

The boy's good-looking face was still badly bruised, and he stood with a protective list toward his left side. Ohara threw him a lead. "Tell us about the accident."

"Yes." Kenji wet his lips and hesitated.

"Did you report it?" Washington asked, putting on the pressure.

"No...I mean...I was hurt but it wasn't a car accident like I told Mr. Konecko."

"Why did you lie to him? He thinks a lot of you." Ohara was content to let Washington carry the ball. He was doing fine.

Kenji looked down at his hands. "I—it was a fight. I didn't want him to know. He doesn't like fighting. I was afraid I'd lose my job."

"What was the fight about?" Ohara probed. Kenji must be wondering how they'd tumbled to him, but he'd kept his nerve and had a story ready.

"I owed somebody money. He sent this guy to collect."

"Loan shark?" Washington was helpful.

"Something like that."

"When did it happen? Where?" Washington wasn't giving him time to think up anything fancy.

"Last Thursday...after work. The guy picked me up, made me get in his car—"

"Any witnesses?"

"Er...no, it was dark. I told him I couldn't pay any more for a while. Then he took me to an alley, I don't remember where, and beat me up." Kenji's eyes grew anxious. "I don't know why you're here. You couldn't have known—"

Ohara took out Morgan's picture. "Do you know this man?"

Kenji barely looked before he answered. "No. Who is he?"

"His name's Roy Morgan. You say you never met him?"

Kenji shook his head, his face tight.

"We have a witness who saw you talking to him."

The boy rallied. "Let me see the picture again." He studied Morgan's face for a moment, then said, "I think I remember. We talked at St. Jude's Carnival for a minute."

"Anyone with you?"

"Yes, my girl. This guy won a teddy bear and gave it to her. I said thanks, that's all."

"You never saw him again?"

"No, why should I?"

"He's dead," Washington said. "Somebody stabbed him."

"Oh." Kenji waited a moment, then looked toward the shop. "Is there anything else?"

"Yes." Washington took out his notebook. "Care to give us a description of the guy who beat you up?"

Panic showed in Kenji's eyes. "No...I mean, he was just a big guy...I was too scared."

Washington played out the scene. "Aren't you afraid he'll come back?"

The boy shrugged, his face pale under the livid bruises.

"That's it then," Ohara said. Released, Kenji hurried back into the shop.

As they watched him go, Washington sighed. "He's not stupid. It would be hard to prove or disprove his story. Wonder why he came over to us after he'd run out of the shop?"

[105]

"Two reasons. He wanted to plant his new story where Konecko couldn't hear and he didn't want us to go to his home. That's what's interesting."

When they got back to the car Ohara checked by radio for messages. There was only one: Morgan's car had been found. He took down an address. "Let's go, Ted. That's not far from Hokey's Place."

XVI

Morgan's dark blue Chevy stood in the far corner of a library parking lot, partially concealed by the cascading branches of a willow tree. An accumulation of dust, leaves and bird droppings attested to its lonely vigil. It was unlocked, and the interior was empty of the usual personalizing trivia.

Washington radioed for the tow truck while Ohara went into the library. According to the report, Miss Gaskell, the head librarian, had called in about the abandoned car. She was a spare, gray-haired woman who silently examined his ID, then invited him into her tiny office. Her eyes, bright behind their granny glasses, evaluated him as they might a new book.

Restraining an impulse to whisper, Ohara asked, "When did you first notice the car, Miss Gaskell?"

"Last Thursday about five-thirty when the young man parked it."

Mentally, Ohara blessed all conscientious librarians. "Would you tell me about it?"

"I was working in the periodical room, which overlooks the parking lot. We discourage parking at the corner to prevent damage to the tree. I intended to speak to the driver when he came into the library, but he didn't come in. He looked like a nice young man, not the kind to use our parking lot when he wasn't visiting the library."

Once again, Ohara noted, someone had described Morgan as a "nice young man." Without comment, he showed her Morgan's picture. "Would this be the man?"

"That looks like him."

"Did you see where he went?"

"No. That wasn't possible."

"Is there anything else you can tell me?"

"When I looked out later, I saw another young man by the car. He was starting to open the hood so I hammered on the window. Right away he jumped over the fence and disappeared."

"Would you describe this man?"

"Ordinary looking, from what I could see, with longish hair not too clean I'm afraid. He looked pale and thin."

"What was he wearing?"

"Jeans and a long-sleeved black shirt."

"I understand you didn't call in until Monday. Why was that?"

Miss Gaskell's face reddened in embarrassment. "I should have called sooner, but just at closing time we had some problems that needed all my attention. Friday I was out sick. We're closed Saturdays now. Monday morning when I came to work, I saw the car still in the lot, so I called. I wonder why that young man abandoned his car?"

Ohara chose his words with care. "He was killed, Miss Gaskell."

"Oh, how sad." Miss Gaskell's brown eyes misted with sudden tears. She took off her glasses and cleaned them with a spotless white handkerchief. Death was an unexpected intrusion into the quiet haven of her library.

Ohara stood up. "Thank you, Miss Gaskell. If you should think of anything else, please get in touch with me." He handed her his card.

When he left the library, the tow truck was just pulling in. Washington gave instructions, then came over to where Ohara waited. "Get anything?"

Ohara gave him the latest gleanings. Washington was thoughtful. "Well, wherever Morgan was going it wasn't far, and he didn't want his car noticed. We could check the block."

They walked to the driveway of the parking lot and stood looking up and down the street. A flash of color drew Ohara's attention. "I don't think Morgan went much farther than that, Ted." He pointed to the left halfway down the block where a hedge of bright pink oleanders almost shouted its presence.

"You know," Washington said as they walked toward it, "until now I didn't think we had a chance to trace that pink petal we found on Morgan."

The hedge extended from a small alley to the corner, forming a dense screen for the first small house. "What's the address Kenji gave for the Kubota house?" Ohara asked.

Washington looked at his notebook. "112 Willow." They continued on to the corner where a leaning street sign read "Willow." The house bedecked with the pink oleander hedge was number 112. "It's looking good, Sam. Morgan came here to see the Kubota girl."

"Good, but not solid enough. We'd better start ringing doorbells. You take this side; I'll check the alley and the houses opposite."

"Back to pounding the pavement." Washington grinned and started off. Ohara retraced his steps past the oleander hedge to where it turned into the small alley. Its flowery screen extended as far as the yard gate attached to a frame garage. When he reached the chest-high gate, he found himself looking into a fairy-tale Japanese garden complete with beautiful maiden. As he looked, the maiden turned and saw him. It was Yumi, looking more like a painting than ever in a pale pink dress that hung loosely from her shoulders in cool, graceful folds.

For a moment she stared blankly, then came toward him hands outstretched, smiling in the way he hadn't been able to forget. She opened the gate and gestured him to come into the yard.

He hesitated, but she impatiently took him by the hand and settled the matter. She led the way toward an old-fashioned glider near the house; he followed willingly.

Her black hair hung long and loose from a coil on top of her head. A gold *kanzashi* pinned a spray of pink oleander above her ear. Thin gold bangles slid along her arms as she moved. Her hand in his was warm and soft. She let go to push him gently down onto the glider, then with a graceful gesture indicated that he should wait.

She ran toward the small garage and disappeared inside. Through the opened door Ohara could see the edge of a long table stacked with doll cases. In a short time she was back, the small doll he had found in Morgan's apartment cupped in her hands. She sat down beside him and held it out, whole again. He could scarcely see the join where the tiny neck had been snapped in two.

He started to say thank you but caught himself in time. Laying the doll on the glider, he stood up and bowed his appreciation. Yumi acknowledged it with a gentle sideways motion of her head. He could see that she was pleased.

She stood looking up at him, her eyes openly admiring. Expressing what she felt was instinctive and natural to her. She studied his face, then moved to his shoulders. Smiling, she spread her arms wide spanning their breadth, totally unaware of how desirable she was and how vulnerable. Even the cruel trick nature had played on her could not shadow that beautiful young face. But what drew Ohara most was the shining innocence that cried out for protection from anything crude or ugly.

When he thought of her in Morgan's hands he was filled with rage. It must have shown in his face, because Yumi's dark eyes filled with alarm and questions. Reaching up, she laid her fingers lightly against his cheek. Her touch was cool and unbelievably sensuous. Angry with himself for alarming her, Ohara smiled reassurance. Then to ease the awkward moment, he reached inside his jacket and took out his wallet. Pulling out some bills, he pointed to the doll and offered them to her.

Yumi shook her head and put her hands behind her. When he continued to hold out the bills, she took the wallet, put the money inside and handed it back to him. As he reluctantly put it away she spotted a gold-plated pen clipped to his shirt pocket. Like a child grabbing for a toy, she unclipped it and held it up, running her fingers over the shiny gold surface.

Ohara closed her fingers around it, indicating that she should keep it. Her face glowed with pleasure. The bright brilliance of gold must appeal to her, he thought, noting again her gold bracelets and gold *kanzashi*. Then an idea spawned in his mind, one that the policeman in him could not ignore. From his pocket he took out the gold bicycle charm and held it out for her to see.

It aroused no reaction in her other than pleasure; she reached for it at once. But Ohara closed his fist and shook his head. He opened his fingers and pointed to himself, then to the charm, hoping she understood. With a sigh she nodded and laid one finger on Ohara's chest. No one could have made "yours" more plain.

Yumi stared at the charm without attempting to touch it, then signing to him to wait, she jumped up and ran into the house. A few minutes later she returned with a large Japanese-style lunch box, a black lacquered *obento*. When she took off the cover, however, it did not contain the usual Japanese cold lunch. The first layer held a jumble of buttons, small combs and ribbons. She set this aside. The second layer was a collection of snapshots and pictures cut from magazines. In her excitement she spilled the contents on the ground. As Ohara helped to pick them up he studied the

[111]

small fragments of her identity. Among the pictures of flowers and small furry animals, he looked longest at the few snapshots that were windows into Yumi's life: Yumi as a baby, Yumi as a toddler in her first kimono, her mother and father, a birthday party, Yumi holding her certificate as a doll maker, Yumi at the park standing between two young boys, one of whom looked like Kenji.

The third layer contained mostly beads and bracelets. She rummaged around with her fingers until she found what she wanted. Triumphantly she held it out. It was a gold charm similar to the one he held. This one was a miniature violin. Ohara stared at it, his mouth going dry. Then unexpectedly Yumi picked up his hand, put the charm in his palm beside the other and closed his fingers around it. She pointed to Ohara and smiled, proud to have given him a gift as he had given one to her.

He opened his palm and turned the little charm over. It was engraved as were the others. This one read "L.A. 6.10.76," just before Morgan had been sent to Folsom. In all innocence she'd given him a piece of evidence that could condemn her. She'd probably kept it because of the pretty shining gold. Unwillingly his eyes went up to the gold *kanzashi* in her hair.

Yumi noticed his glance and misinterpreted it. She reached up and pulled out the *kanzashi*, then handed him the sprig of oleander. Frozen, he watched her white fingers replace the dagger-sharp hairpin in the coil of her hair. He looked down at the pink flower in his palm and tried to smile. Yumi took the small spray of blossoms from him and tucked it into the buttonhole of his lapel. She looked at him a moment with an indecipherable expression in her eyes, then leaned over and kissed him lightly on the cheek.

Just past her shoulder Ohara saw Washington starting to come in through the back gate and motioned to him to stay where he was. Yumi, busy putting her treasure box back together again, did not notice.

Looking at her calm innocent face, Ohara thought about what he now had to do. It would make him as much a violator as Morgan. He put his hand in his jacket pocket, then hesitated. Yumi looked up, saw his movement and reached for the pocket, her face bright with the anticipation of a new surprise. Her fingers squirmed beneath his and teased the picture out, almost tearing it in the process.

She looked at it blankly for a moment, showing neither recognition nor concealment. With relief he guessed that some mercy had blanked everything out of her mind, perhaps even murder. Then her hand holding the picture began to tremble, and chilling incomprehensible sounds came from her throat. She threw the picture to the ground, rubbing her hands frantically against her dress as she stared at it in horror. Then she began to scream, ear-piercing shrieks of terror that brought Washington over on the run.

Hating himself, Ohara slapped her sharply across the face to stem her mounting hysteria. She cowered away from him like a frightened animal, stunned into hiccupping sobs. Her body began to shiver. Ohara pulled her into his arms, pressed her head against his shoulder and stroked her hair, calming her as he might a child, saying the soothing useless words she could not hear. Washington started to speak, but above Yumi's bent head he saw the bitter rage in Ohara's face and kept silent.

XVII

"Yumi! What happen my Yumi?"

Mrs. Kubota's frantic voice shrilled at them as she came in a clumsy, jolting run down the back porch steps, with Kenji just behind her. She pulled her daughter from Ohara's arms and anxiously scanned the girl's tear-stained face.

"What's going on here?" Kenji demanded.

"I'm sorry," Ohara answered. "I showed Yumi Morgan's picture." He bent down and picked up the picture from the ground where Yumi had thrown it.

"You've no right to force your way in here and frighten a helpless girl. Do you have a warrant?"

"No, I don't have a warrant, but I didn't force my way in here. Yumi saw me outside in the alley, and invited me in to give me this." Ohara walked over to the glider and picked up the mended doll.

"Well, you can go now, both of you. We know our rights."

From the shelter of her mother's arms. Yumi looked anxiously from one to the other, trying to understand what was happening. Then she caught sight of the picture in Ohara's hand. She snatched at it and ran toward Kenji. Excitedly she pointed to the man in the picture, then raised her fists and pretended to batter Kenji's head and shoulders, looking back at Ohara to be sure he understood her meaning. She pointed once again to the picture, then softly stroked the bruises on Kenji's face.

"If I hadn't seen it, I'd never have believed it," Washington said softly. "She's telling us it was Morgan who beat you up, Kimura. That's true, isn't it?"

Mrs. Kubotas's hand flew to her mouth in alarm. Kenji,

shaken, answered, "Yes." His eyes were fixed on Mrs. Kubota in silent appeal.

"Perhaps you'd rather talk to us at the station," Ohara said. "It might be better for everyone." His glance rested on Yumi.

Fear flooded Kenji's face. Mrs. Kubota came over to him and clutched his arm, her lips trembling. Kenji patted her shoulder. "It will be all right, *O Fukuro*, don't worry."

When Ohara heard "*O Fukuro*," the old-style, tender Japanese for mother, he knew the strength of the bond between the woman and the boy. Kenji was the son of her heart, if not her body.

Kenji turned for a moment to Yumi and, smiling gently, took her hands in his in a silent communication of reassurance. Her eyes questioned his a moment, then she stood on tiptoe and kissed his bruised cheek. The three men walked to the alley gate and let themselves out. Yumi ran after them as far as the fence, waving goodbye like a little child. They all waved back. Only Mrs. Kubota's stifled sobs broke the heavy silence.

As they drove past the house Ohara noticed an elderly black Buick parked at the curb. "Your car, Kenji?" he asked.

"No. It's Mrs. Kubota's. I sometimes drive it to work. Tonight I picked her up at the store to come home for supper. We've been doing that lately."

Washington glanced at Ohara. The car was similar to the one a neighbor had observed at the place Morgan's body had been found. He would have it picked up and checked out.

When they reached the station they took Kenji to an empty office and asked him to wait a moment. Outside, Ohara turned to Washington. "Did you turn up anything in the neighborhood, Ted?"

"Pay dirt. Nobody saw Morgan, but some kids playing down the block saw Kenji go in before six, and Mrs. Kubota not long afterward. They remembered because she gave them some candy from the store. A neighbor said that an old lady knocked at the door a few minutes after six. She made quite a fuss, banging and hollering, but no one let her in and she had to go away."

"That must have been the old woman who was complaining about it when I was at the grocery."

Ohara reached into his pocket for the violin charm and handed it to Washington. "I got this from Yumi."

"Just like the others," Washington murmured, then read the date. "So Yumi had it. How did you get it?"

Ohara's face was bleak. "I showed her the other one, the bicycle, and she ran into the house to get me this one. It meant nothing to her. It was just a pretty shiny trinket."

"You can bet Morgan didn't give it to her," Washington said, then, seeing Ohara's mouth tighten, wished he hadn't. "Anyway, I'd like to put this date on the computer."

"Do it," Ohara said. "But first I want to show it to Kenji. Let's go talk to him."

When they entered with a police stenographer, the boy stiffened and inched forward on his chair. "Would you like a cigarette?" Ohara asked.

"No, thank you."

"Would you like a lawyer present?"

"No, I just want to get this over."

"That's good," Ohara said, and read him his rights. Taking the charm out of his pocket, he laid it on the table in front of Kenji. "Ever see this before?"

As a bombshell it failed to go off. Kenji looked at the gold charm, surprised. "No, I never saw it before."

His surprise seemed genuine. Ohara put the charm away and settled back to listen. "Now tell us what really happened to you."

"Well, Thursdays I usually get home before six. Yumi waits for me and we cook supper for Mama together. That

[117]

Thursday, Yumi wasn't in the house or the yard, so I went to her workshop in the garage."

He paused a moment, then went on. "When I opened the door...the man from the carnival, Morgan, had Yumi down on the floor. Her clothes were almost torn off and he had his hands around her throat. I shouted and ran at him. I beat on his back and his head to make him let go of her. Finally he jumped up and went for me karate-style. He was smiling as if it was a game. I knew I couldn't beat him, but I had to give Yumi a chance to get away." Kenji stopped and wet his lips, his eyes on his fists clenched on the table in front of him. After a deep, shuddering breath he went on. "He dropped me with a kick under the ribs and when I went down he was right on top of me, beating on my head and face. He kept it up until I blacked out. Last thing I remember was the way he was laughing."

He eyed Ohara and waited. It was Washington who spoke. "Then since you had blacked out you don't really know what else happened? Morgan could have been killed right there by Yumi, or maybe Mrs. Kubota."

Kenji tensed, his face desperate. "No...there's more. I blacked out only for a second. Then I rolled over, away from him. But he still came after me. It happened so fast...it's hard to get it all straight. I saw Yumi's *kanzashi* on the floor near my hand...I grabbed for it and struck him...and he fell over dead."

"So you killed Morgan." Washington dropped the words into the silence. "Is that what you're telling us?"

"I had to...it was self-defense."

Ohara stared at him for a moment, then said, "As you say, Kenji, everything happened pretty fast. I'd like to try to visualize it better. Mr. Washington, here, will pretend to be Morgan coming after you. Here, use this pencil as the *kanzashi*."

[118]

Ohara rolled a pencil toward Kenji, who caught it at the table edge with his right hand. "Now show us just how you did it."

Kenji dropped to his knees, fighting back a groan. He kept the pencil in his right fist. "I was like this," he said.

"And how was Morgan standing?"

"He was sort of bent over...with his hand raised to chop me."

Washington assumed the position, then moved as if to strike. Kenji lunged upward with the pencil, aiming for the throat but coming closer to the jawline. The movement made him gasp with pain.

Washington helped him to his feet and into the chair. "Sorry," Ohara said. "You had to kill him in self-defense. Is that right?"

A flicker of hope showed in Kenji's eyes. "Yes...self-defense."

"Why didn't you call the police afterward? It being self-defense, you would have had no problems."

Kenji hesitated a moment, then said, "We couldn't because of Yumi. All the questions...we were afraid for her..."

"Who is 'we'?" Washington asked.

"I had to tell Mama when she came. Yumi was hysterical. It was very bad. That's why we didn't call the police."

That was probably the truth, Ohara thought, then said, "What did you do?"

"Mama gave Yumi medicine to make her sleep and put her to bed. That was the best way, we thought."

"Then what?" Washington cut in. "Morgan's body must have been some problem."

Kenji nodded, looking miserable. "Late that night, I put it in the car and took it to a deserted street that had a lot of bushes. I put it there."

Ohara glanced over at Washington. "I guess that makes everything clear. When your statement is transcribed, we'll bring it to you to sign."

"Then can I go home?"

"No. We're going to have to book you."

Kenji looked at them in disbelief, panic in his eyes. "Why? You said it was self-defense. I told you he was trying to kill me...maybe Yumi, too..."

"That's true," Ohara said, "but you disposed of the body without notifying the police and destroyed evidence. We have to hold you for that."

Kenji slumped back in his chair and closed his eyes. He'd thought he was home free, but he wasn't. "I'll have to call Mama. She'll be worried."

"We'll arrange for that after your statement is signed. You can wait here."

Outside in the hall when the door had closed, Washington asked, "How shall we book him?"

"A technical charge—interfering with evidence, unlawful transportation of a dead body."

Washington looked troubled. "Do you really buy that self-defense bit? Somehow I can't see a guy like Morgan letting himself get caught that way. He'd have to be taken unawares."

"I don't buy it either, Ted, with good reason. You didn't see the final autopsy report, but it shows that Morgan was killed from behind by a left-handed person."

"And Kenji came at me with his right, and from the front."

"Yes."

"Then he's protecting the girl, or Mama, if she walked in on it. Is she left-handed?"

"Yes," Ohara answered, seeing that small square left hand smoothing Yumi's hair, clutching desperately at Kenji's arm.

"Then why not bring her in?"

"I don't want to, not yet."

[120]

Ted opened his mouth to argue, then shut it again. For just a moment he wondered if Ohara would have hesitated if the people hadn't been Japanese, if they'd been black, for example. Ohara was staring at him, almost as if he'd guessed his thoughts. The look in the older man's black eyes was diamond hard.

Washington smiled his big easy smile and lightly touched Ohara's shoulder. "Whatever you say, partner." He glanced at his watch. "Quittin' time, boss, OK?"

When Ohara nodded, he smiled and headed down the corridor like a man with nothing more on his mind than home and a cold beer.

Ohara watched him go. Technically, Ted was right. It was simply good procedure to question the Kubotas promptly. But it was no longer a by-the-book case. All his life he'd recognized the law as the arbiter of justice. It would have been right, even satisfying, to bring Morgan to justice, but not an old woman or a fragile, mentally slow girl. They were the victims, not the criminals. He walked toward his office, knowing he'd do what he had to do. But if there was a way to make it easier on Yumi, he'd find it.

XVIII

HANA Kubota looked around her small store with a sense of pride. Shig had washed the windows and was now straightening the shelves of canned goods. She'd arranged the vegetable bins herself, as she loved to do. They looked fresh and inviting.

In the early afternoon between customers, she'd worked on her accounts, so they were in order, too. That morning she'd engaged a lawyer for Kenji, a good one. Mr. Chuman was expensive but his reputation for success was well known in the Japanese community.

She ran her hand across the smooth wood of the old-fashioned counter, taking comfort in the feel of it. The little store had done well by them all these years. She felt suddenly very lonely and very tired; in another minute she'd be crying. She pressed her fingers against her lips to still their quivering, then called to the boy straightening shelves in the corner. "Come here, Shig, *dozo*. I have a job for you."

A heavy sigh floated up from behind the soup cans, but presently Shig ambled over to the counter. She smiled at him. "I must go home early today. You will take charge."

Shig wondered what was up. Maybe she was going to the jail to see Kenji. "Sure, Mrs. Kubota, anything you say."

Hana smiled. "You are a good boy, Shig. Time you had a nice bonus, yes?"

This had not happened before. Shig could hardly believe his good luck but, sure enough, she opened the register and handed him a twenty-dollar bill. "Gee, thanks, Mrs. Kubota. I'll take good care of the store. Don't worry about a thing."

She nodded and fished under the counter for her worn

leather handbag. Then she filled a small paper bag with a handful of candy bars and headed for the door.

As she walked slowly down the street, Hana relished the hot afternoon sun on her shoulders. She did not hurry, but walked purposefully along. So many times she'd gone down this street, seeing nothing. Now each detail stood out with cameo clarity...a crack in the pavement...Mrs. Ricardo's bedraggled geraniums...a tricycle abandoned by the curb. She wondered if the children would be waiting this early for their treat from the store.

They spotted her half a block away and came running. Smiling, she emptied the brown paper bag, doling candy into each grubby hand. The kids ran off with their loot and she walked on. The neighborhood had changed since she and Isao had first bought their house. If he'd lived, so many things might have been different. But she'd done the best she could. All that was left was to finish everything honorably.

As she turned up the path to her house, she stopped to pull a weed, tucking it carefully into her pocketbook. She stood a moment gazing at the oleanders, enjoying the rich pink color. Sighing, she walked up the steps and let herself into the house.

She went straight to the kitchen. Looking out the window over the sink, she saw Yumi going into the workshop. That was good; there were many things to do. She went next into the small, sparsely furnished living room to stand before a memorial shrine of dark polished wood. The picture of her husband, Isao, was banked with pink oleander blossoms arranged by Yumi. Hana clapped her hands three times and bowed her head. After a moment she looked up at the face that was part of another life.

With reverent hands she opened the small doors of the shrine and touched the wooden box placed beneath the gold memorial plaque. It held the precious ashes, waiting to go back with her to Japan someday, for burial in Isao's home village. "*Gomen nasai*," she whispered. "Now I cannot take you home." The pent-up tears overflowed.

After a moment she wiped her eyes and gently closed the doors of the shrine. Then she sat down at her husband's roll-top desk and from one of the many pigeonholes she took out paper and pen. It was a felt-tipped pen; the columns of Japanese characters flowed effortlessly down the paper. What she had to write she could not express adequately in English. Only Japanese, with its clear definition of each nuance of feeling, could say it all. She was glad to know the Japanese officer would read her words and understand.

When she had finished she found a large envelope. She put in the closely written sheets and sealed it firmly. Taking a small card from her purse, she carefully copied onto the front of the envelope: "Police Officer Isamu Ohara."

It had taken more time than she had thought. She would have to hurry now. Carrying the letter, she went upstairs to her bedroom and laid it on her dresser. From the closet shelf she lifted down a black lacquer box. It was filled with herbal medicines unknown to American pharmacies; she was skilled in their use. A small vial, three-quarters full of a dark green liquid, was the one she selected. A few drops could heal, more than that could kill. She put the box back on the closet shelf and, dropping the vial into her pocket, she went downstairs to the kitchen to begin preparing a meal. She took out food for a special meal that Yumi loved. Looking out of the window she saw her daughter come out of the workroom and waved. Yumi waved back in pleased surprise and headed for the house.

As always she greeted her mother with a loving hug. Hana shut her eyes, squeezing back the tears, remembering the green vial in her pocket. Pulling Yumi closer, she stroked her hair and face, murmuring "*Akachan...Akachan,*" the long-ago baby name. Yumi looked up, surprised. Her mother was not usually demonstrative. After a moment, Hana motioned with her normal brusqueness at the waiting vegetables.

Yumi took up a knife and began to prepare them. She fixed the rice and set out some fruit. Hana busied herself with the fish and made the sauce. When the meal was ready, Hana sent Yumi to fetch the best teacups from the dining room cabinet. While the girl was gone, she filled two bowls with rice and two more with fish and vegetables. For just a second she hesitated. Then, sighing, she uncorked the green vial and poured it over Yumi's bowl. She just had time to toss the empty vial in the garbage can when her daughter returned with the teacups. They sat down to supper.

Yumi ate with great enjoyment, as she did everything, pausing every now and then to stroke her mother's hand in affectionate thanks for her favorite supper. Hana's hand burned at the touch as she watched her daughter swallow the savory, highly spiced food in which the contents of the green vial went undetected.

She barely touched her own food, but watched Yumi's face, her eyes caressing it with so much love she thought her heart would burst. Once Yumi looked up and saw that her mother seemed sad. She stopped eating to reach over and pat the pale, tired-looking face, then smiled and gestured to her mother's untouched food. Obediently Hana spooned a mouthful between her lips. She couldn't even taste it.

The poison she had chosen was gentle and slow-acting. There would be no pain. Soon Yumi would feel sleepy and want to take a nap. Then she would drift from sleep to death and no one would be able to hurt her anymore. Beyond this Hana refused to think.

As they finished up the dishes, Yumi yawned and rubbed

her eyes. At once Hana was beside her, cradling the drowsy girl in her arms. Pointing upstairs, she pantomimed sleep by pillowing her head against her folded hands. Gently smiling, Yumi nodded. Then, supported in Hana's strong arms, she allowed herself to be led up to bed like a sleepy child.

With a soft sound of comfort Yumi snuggled down into her familiar bed. Lovingly Hana smoothed her pillow and drew a soft white wool shawl over her. Yumi did not move or open her eyes. She sighed deeply once and slipped further into sleep.

Hana watched her a few minutes. It had been so simple, and yet so hard to do. Now, after a quiet sleep free from pain or anguish, her child would be safe. Hana stooped and kissed the pale, beautiful face, touched the soft hair that fanned against the pillow, then left the room and closed the door behind her.

Suddenly weak, she leaned against the wall and began to tremble. What kind of mother would kill her own child? It was terrible beyond belief, but there was no other way. These last days she'd been living in terror. For just a little time, reading in the paper that the police were looking somewhere else, she had thought they'd be safe. But from the day the Japanese detective had come to the store, she had known he'd find out. When they arrested Kenji, there was no more hope. She knew he would sacrifice himself to save them, but she could not let that happen. Eventually they'd take Yumi and lock her away. She would die alone and frightened, cut off from all who loved her. It was better this way.

Kenji would have no need to lie for them. He would be free. He'd been a son to her and she loved him as her own. The money she had so carefully saved would see him through medical school. She had arranged with the lawyer for a proper will. Little Kenji would become Dr. Kimura; of that she felt proud already.

The thought gave her the strength she needed for what must still be done. Going into the bathroom she washed her body thoroughly, taking care to leave everything neat behind her. In her bedroom she took out her best kimono of gray silk, laid it on the bed, then brushed and recoiled her hair. Next she put on a spotless white cotton undergarment, adjusting the folds at the throat to perfect smoothness. From the drawer she picked out a pair of white *tabi* and put them on her small, calloused feet. She slid her arms into her kimono, folding the gray silk across her body. Out of habit she folded it left side over right, then, remembering, she refolded it, right over left, as appropriate for death.

This done, she tied it with a braided cord and took her formal obi of black and silver brocade out of its tissue paper wrappings. With practiced ease she positioned its stiff confining folds. From an ivory box on the dresser she drew her grandmother's dagger-sharp *kanzashi*. Slowly, because her hands trembled, she placed it in the knot of her hair. In the mirror her squat, heavy body looked suddenly dignified, almost graceful.

Picking up the letter she had prepared, she went downstairs. Once more she stood before the small shrine and bowed three times. She knew that what must be done should be done here. But she wasn't sure she could carry out the ritual without faltering. It was best to make doubly sure.

She went next to the linen closet and took out a freshly laundered sheet, which she carried into the kitchen and spread out on the floor near the stove. On one corner she laid the letter addressed to Ohara. Then she closed the kitchen door and wadded dish towels at the sill and more at the back door and the windows. Everything was now ready.

After blowing out the pilot flames, she turned all the gas jets on full and opened the oven door. Kneeling down in the center of the white sheet, she carefully straightened the folds of her kimono around her. Then she took the *kanzashi* out of her hair and laid it on the sheet in front of her.

The sight of the needle-sharp blade, ready and waiting, chilled her. This was no ordinary *kanzashi*. It was a lethal weapon, made many years ago to protect a woman's honor. In other times her family had been well-to-do and worthy of respect. Only in America had she been a storekeeper. Tradition still bound her as firmly as the obi at her waist; neither would allow her to bend from the upright way.

She tried to pray, but with little hope of forgiveness. What she had done was unforgivable, but she had saved Yumi and Kenji, the only two in the world who mattered to her.

Slowly she reached down and picked up the *kanzashi*.

As a child she'd listened in awe and admiration to her mother's stories of how in times past, women of Japan had chosen death before dishonor. It didn't matter that it was no longer so. She wished she had the proper second standing behind her to finish the death stroke, should she fail. The gas would have to do.

With the same firm movements so characteristic of her nature, she raised the *kanzashi* in both hands, touched the blade to her forehead, then, without hesitation, plunged it deep into her throat.

The pain was agonizing and the bright blood spurted out onto the white linen folds at her throat. She fell forward, willing herself into the mercy of death. As she yielded to the engulfing waves of darkness, her last conscious thought was of Isao's faded picture beside the little shrine.

She never heard the pounding on the door.

XIX

LATER Ohara would blame himself for not sensing what kind of woman Hana Kubota really was. After Kenji's confession he had gone home, putting off bringing in the Kubotas until the next day. All evening he'd doubted the wisdom of his decision.

After a more or less sleepless night, he lay watching the early morning light make gray oblongs of the bedroom windows. Before the day was over, he would do what had to be done, but first he would attempt to balance the scales of justice a little. He would make the case against Morgan, insofar as he was able. It would not help the two young girls so callously represented by Morgan's gold charms, but at least the cases would be closed. It might make a difference to the Kubotas, too.

The best practical help he could offer Yumi would be Dr. Harry Hondo. The thought of her being taken from her small secure world and committed to the impersonal custody of a county mental asylum haunted him. He could picture the light going out of her lovely eyes and her bright smile fading into a vacant stare.

Dr. Harry Hondo, a brilliant psychiatrist and criminal psychologist, was a boyhood friend. He'd helped a host of lame ducks like Yumi; his "special cases," he called them. They'd turned to him for help and found it, whether they could pay or not. They were his greatest satisfaction

Heartened by the decision and impatient for day to begin, Ohara resigned himself to watching the gray oblongs of light turn gold with the sun. Still the need to clear his mind and shake his body loose was urgent; he knew the remedy. He would go to Ojiisan's *dojo* for a workout. In Japan practice began at five A.M., but in concession to Western self-indulgence Ojiisan Takahashi opened the *dojo* at six-thirty.

He slipped out of bed and began to dress. As he pulled his *gi* from the closet shelf Peggy awoke. Drowsily she offered to fix breakfast but he assured her he wanted nothing, kissed her and tucked her in again. "Say hello to Ojiisan," she muttered into the pillow.

When Ohara arrived at the *dojo* Peggy's grandfather was already there instructing a new student. Erect and vigorous for all his seventy-five years, Master Takahashi was present every morning except Sunday to teach Aikido, not leaving it to the younger instructors. He still moved about the floor with the effortless grace Ohara had admired years ago.

As Ohara changed his clothes, he noticed that the wound from Flaco's knife was healing nicely. Though it was surprisingly small, an inch or so either way would have ripped muscles and nerves, leaving his arm useless. He'd been lucky, thanks to Ted Washington—something he wouldn't forget.

After a few minutes of warmup, he joined the two young brown belts working out on the mat. His arm pained him considerably, but he ignored it and enjoyed the new surge of energy released by the exercise. The necessary concentration of *ki* eased the turmoil of his thoughts and he felt whole again.

Afterwards, Ojiisan invited him into his private *tatami* room in the rear of the *dojo* and served him tea in his favorite small brown cup. Ohara held it in his hands, enjoying, as was intended, the perfection of the thick antique glaze, soothing to the touch as the simplicity of the room soothed the eye. The *tokonomo* scroll in Ojiisan's graceful calligraphy proclaimed "Mind and Body Are One." Beneath it in a bamboo vase a flower arrangement of three glowing red asters was a gentle reminder of the universal harmony of heaven, man and earth, the criterion of true happiness. Looking at it, Ohara thought with sadness that he didn't often see that harmony in his line of work.

Ojiisan asked after his granddaughter and the children. Then, placing his teacup on the lacquer tray between them, he studied Ohara carefully. Above his dark kimono his face was serene and his eyes were filled with tranquility. "You are unhappy, Isamu," he said in his soft yet firm voice.

Ohara sighed. "In my work, Ojiisan, right is sometimes wrong, and wrong often appears right. I have such a problem now."

The old man smiled. "It is often so in this life, Isamu. Be happy that you have the wisdom to know it. Many do not, so they struggle and suffer painfully. But as in Aikido, you must let what will come of itself come."

It was like the old days when Master Takahashi had taught him more than the martial art of Aikido. After a moment Ojiisan said, "Rest here if you wish, Isamu. I have a student waiting." In one supple movement he was on his feet. Motioning to Ohara to remain seated, he left the room.

Ohara sipped at his tea, thinking that Ojiisan was right. What will come of itself he must let come. Only the truth need concern him, even if it was not always simple to understand or accept. He let the peace of the room fill him, no longer trying to ignore the now-throbbing pain in his arm, but accepting it as being another kind of truth. As he did, his mind became so centered on one singular thought that he was no longer even aware of the pain. With this thought as a guide he went over the case again, realizing as he did so that an idea had presented itself twice before and he hadn't considered it.

When he left the *dojo* he went directly to his office and

[133]

called Harry Hondo. The first available time was four-thirty, which suited Ohara perfectly. He had a lot of other things to do.

Next he took the morgue photographs of Morgan from his desk and studied them until he found one which suited his purpose. He took it over to the photo lab and asked for a blowup. He also asked that a second photograph be taken. Used to peculiar requests, they obliged and promised to send the pictures over when they were ready.

When he got back to his desk, Washington was already there poring over a computer printout from Records. "Hi, Sam," Washington said, full of purpose. "Take a look at this. Here's the total number of unsolved rape-murder cases discovered in the Los Angeles area on or about June 10, 1976."

"You're thinking my thoughts two jumps ahead," Ohara said as he bent over the printout. There were ten that fitted the time frame. Of these, three were small children, one a woman in her eighties, two women over thirty. None of these matched Morgan's pattern, but the four remaining were all possibles. It would be necessary to contact the individual investigating officers for details.

When they pinpointed the cases, one was in the San Fernando Valley, one in Santa Monica, one in the Los Feliz area and one in Hollywood. "I have two other stops to make and a four-thirty appointment," Ohara said. "I can fit the Los Feliz area in but I'd be grateful if you could take the others."

"No sweat," Washington answered and reached for the phone. They were lucky. The case officers concerned were available, so he made the appointments. "If none of these proves out, we could still try the others. Morgan might have changed his style."

"Good idea," Ohara agreed. "Whatever happens, I want you to meet me in front of the Kubota Grocery about five-forty-five. It's time to get this thing rolled up."

"Right." Washington picked up the addresses and headed for the door.

Ohara had said nothing to him about the rather startling idea that had come to him at the *dojo*, feeling it was still too nebulous. He needed something more solid on which to build. It was a big "if," and however it went the due process of law still lay like a shadow over the Kubotas.

As he walked down the hall on his way out, he noticed that Reilly was in his office. Ohara went in on the chance that he could get what he needed on Morgan. Reilly was cordial but he was in a hurry. "I'm just leaving for a conference at the Federal Bureau, Sam. What can I do for you?"

"I'm trying to tie up a few loose ends on the Morgan case. Did you find Chino?"

"The man who was Flaco's alibi? Yes, but we're drying him out now; he isn't coherent enough to talk to you. I have a preliminary statement, such as it is, if that would help."

"I'd like to see it."

"OK, Sam, on my way out I'll have Bea bring it in to you."

After the secretary brought the file, Ohara went over it at Reilly's desk. When he was finished he sat a few minutes thinking hard, then returned it. The same uneasy feeling of the night before gnawed at him. He called the lab, he needed those pictures now. Luckily they were just finished. "I'll be right in," he said.

The photographs were better than he'd hoped, so he lost no time in chasing down Abrams at the morgue and laying them out for his inspection as he outlined his theory.

Thoughtfully the pathologist studied them, then produced another photograph for comparison. "You got a good fortune cookie this time, Charlie Chan. It just could be."

Smiling, Ohara gathered up the photographs, including the one Abrams had brought. "Japanese fortune-telling this time. Charlie Chan had nothing to do with it."

[135]

His next stop was his appointment with Detective Kronski, who'd handled the Los Feliz 1976 rape-murder, one of those that could have been Morgan's. He was a ruddy-faced man with gray hair, more than willing to discuss the case. But when he began to talk about the young victim his face was grim. "I'll never understand how they can do it, and I've seen a lot of them. This little one, her name was Kathy, was only twelve years old. Here, read the details." He handed over the file. "I can't forget them after all these years."

Ohara scanned the reports. It had been a rape-bludgeoning murder, which was out of pattern. She'd had a short kid's haircut, too, again not Morgan's pattern. Ohara could understand how Kronski never forgot these details; they were gruesome. It didn't seem possible that they were describing the body of the bright-eyed youngster whose picture was stapled to the file.

"Think it's your man?" Kronski asked, his eyes sharp.

"No, I'm sorry. Different MO." Ohara handed back the file.

"I always keep hoping. I keep thinking about the son of a bitch trying it again. Poor little tyke was the same age as my granddaughter; looked kind of like her, too."

By four-thirty Ohara was sitting opposite Dr. Harry Hondo in his comfortable Beverly Hills office. The doctor listened quietly while Ohara told him the whole story. "You're a funny kind of cop, Sam," was Harry Hondo's first comment. "The usual procedure is to solve the case and let the chips fall where they may."

"I know…but not this time if I can help it. Maybe I should say, if *you* can help it. Yumi deserves better." Ohara spread his hands in a small empty gesture that was as close to pleading as he could get.

Dr. Hondo took off his rimless glasses and polished them on his handkerchief. His eyes, kind and vulnerable-looking without their glass shield, surveyed his friend. "I'm persuaded. From what you say the girl may not be as retarded as supposed. I wonder why she never received any help. There are schools—"

"Her mother thinks old-style Japan; she's not the type to look for that kind of help. She'd feel it was better to keep Yumi at home, protected, than to put her in the hands of strangers."

"I know what you mean. My mother was old-fashioned Japanese to the bone. How can I help?"

"You may have to volunteer to take Yumi into your custody as your patient. That's why I want you to see her now. Whatever happens, I know you can help her."

"I'd like to try. I knew another one like that—"

"There's something else, Harry," Ohara cut in, his smile apologetic. "I'm going over to see the Kubotas now. If I can't get the truth out of the mother, I'll have to try Yumi. It could be pretty bad. I don't want to do her any damage, so I'd like you standing by. Can you come with me now?"

Harry looked surprised, then checked his calendar. "It should be a new experience, Sam. And I have to admit, after what you've told me, I want to see Yumi."

Ohara smiled. Dr. Hondo was already making plans for his new lame duck.

XX

When Ohara and Dr. Hondo arrived at the Kubota Grocery, Washington met them. "I found what we were looking for, Sam."

"I can use that kind of news," Ohara replied, getting out of the car. "Tell me about it."

"The only case that matches Morgan's MO was out in the Valley—a blond youngster about twelve, last seen walking home from a music lesson. She wasn't found for five days. The body had been stuffed in a culvert along with her violin. There'd been a bad rain so there were no usable prints. But it's got Morgan all over it—she even had long silky hair like the Kubota girl and the child from King City. I'd say the violin charm is as good as a signature."

"Just about," Ohara said. The two men looked at each other in mutual satisfaction.

Harry Hondo, careful not to intrude, found them an interesting study. They were physical opposites with inbred prejudices to reconcile, yet they appeared to have a highly compatible relationship. Belatedly, Ohara made introductions, adding, "Harry Hondo is my good friend, Ted, and one of the best psychiatrists around. I asked him to come along because it may be a bad scene when we talk to Yumi and her mother. He's agreed to take care of Yumi."

"Glad to hear it," Washington said, thinking it was typical of Ohara to work things out that way.

"Let's get going." Ohara led the way into the Kubota Grocery.

They found only Shig, leaning on the counter reading a

magazine. He recognized Ohara and straightened at once. "Hi. You want to ask me more questions?"

"Not just now, Shig," Ohara responded, "but would you please tell Mrs. Kubota we'd like to talk to her."

"She's not here; she left early, about three-thirty."

"Do you know where she went?"

"Nope."

Ohara knew there were several reasons why Hana Kubota might leave the store early, but it bothered him. "Did she say when she'd be back?"

"Nope."

Pushed by a sense of urgency Ohara turned to the others. "Let's try the house."

As they drove to the Kubota house, Washington asked, "Do you think she's on the run?"

"I don't know—she shouldn't have panicked that fast." When they arrived they found someone there before them. Ohara went up the steps to confront an elderly Japanese grandmother-type who was shouting her lungs out at the front door, pausing only for breath and to bang on the door with her cane. She turned to him at last to vent her outrage. Washington appealed to Harry. "What's she saying?"

"The old lady's complaining that this is the second time she's come a long way for her appointment with Kubota-san and been left standing on the porch." After listening a moment he went on. "She says she's not going away this time until someone opens the door. She knows they're in there because one of the neighbors saw Mrs. Kubota come home a long time ago."

The banging began again and Ohara came down the steps looking worried. "I'm going to check out the back. You'd better stay here."

He went around the side of the house. The banging grew louder. Washington looked at Harry, gritting his teeth. "I don't know which'll go first, the door or my eardrums."

[140]

"Leave it to me," Harry said and went up to distract the old lady. Miraculously he stopped her banging and got her to sit down on a porch chair. Sitting beside her, he let her harangue him about her woes.

As Washington started around to the back he heard Ohara shout and the sound of breaking glass. He changed course and in two swift leaps was up the steps. "OK, Grandma, you're going to get your wish." He braced himself and launched an expert kick at the door lock, and the worn old door flew open.

"In here!" Ohara's voice came from his right. He saw a swing door and with difficulty pushed his way through against the wadded dish towels at his feet. The sickly smell of gas enveloped him. "Get the window over the sink! I've turned off the gas."

Washington went to open the window and when he turned back Ohara was bent over the crumpled body of a woman sprawled on a blood-stained sheet, a gold stiletto projecting from her throat. "My God." Washington's voice was almost a whisper. "What did she do to herself?"

Ohara looked up, "Seppuku…hara-kiri…get Harry Hondo in here."

There was no need to call him. Harry was just coming in the door. "I'll get an ambulance," Washington said, and went to find a phone. He was relieved to see the old lady still sitting on the porch peering in, too thunderstruck to interfere. The phone was at the end of the hall. By the time he'd finished his call Ohara was coming out of the kitchen. "How is she?" Washington glanced toward the kitchen.

"Harry's doing what he can. Let's find Yumi."

They checked the downstairs rooms then went upstairs. The last room they looked in was Yumi's. She lay on the bed, a small inert mound under a white shawl. Ohara touched her cheek, lifted her eyelid, then picked her up in his arms and carried her down the stairs. Washington, just behind him, heard his grim comment. "This shouldn't have happened; it was going to be all right."

Just outside the kitchen Ohara stopped and called, "Harry, I've got the girl. She needs help."

Dr. Hondo looked up, still maintaining his firm pressure on the wound in Hana Kubota's neck. She lay on her side with one hand showing beneath the long gray silk sleeve of her kimono, its palm red-stained.

Harry looked at Washington. "Ted, come hold this pressure." When Washington had taken over holding the pad in place, Harry went to Ohara and looked at the girl. "Take her into the other room."

Ohara carried Yumi into the living room and laid her down on the sofa. Dr. Hondo examined her and shook his head. "She's pretty far gone. It all depends on whether or not we can get her to the hospital in time. Do you know what she took?"

"No, but I'll look around. I may find the bottle."

Once again Ohara went upstairs and searched, but found nothing. He came back downstairs and went into the kitchen, where Washington patiently held the pressure on Hana Kubota's neck. The table and the drainboard of the sink were bare of even so much as a glass. He opened the cupboard underneath and found the wastebasket. It held an empty medicine vial which had no odor but bore traces of a sticky green substance. When he turned to take it to Harry, he saw the edge of an envelope almost hidden beneath the crumpled sheet. He picked it up and read the firm, neat writing: "Police Officer Isamu Ohara."

"Looks like a confession." Washington's voice plucked at Ohara's attention. He looked down at Hana Kubota, seeing not the humble little storekeeper but a woman who had lived her life, even to the ultimate moment, according to a code now largely a tradition for the history books. Unconsciously

[142]

he drew himself up in pride and respect, responding to an emotion totally alien to his American background. Watching him, Washington sensed his feeling and in his own way understood it. He no longer noticed the blood seeping out to stain his hands. "Poor soul, she must have been terribly afraid."

"Yes, she was afraid, but not for herself. Only the brave choose this way to die. I should have guessed what she would do; I could have prevented it."

"Maybe," Washington said, "but what gets me is that it should be over a bastard like Morgan. A good lawyer could have got her off."

"You don't understand." Ohara looked down at Hana's strong, square face. "It wasn't over Morgan. She didn't kill him."

XXI

"THAT's not the way I add it up, Sam, but I'm listening." Doubt was plain on Washington's face as he confronted Ohara over Hana Kubota's still body. To him, her attempted suicide spoke for itself. Ohara was holding an envelope that probably contained her confession. So how in hell, he wondered, could Ohara come to the conclusion that she was innocent?

Feet pounding up the front steps put an end to further speculation. The ambulance had arrived and the ensuing turmoil of activity took precedence over everything else. When the patients were ready for transport, Ohara rode with them in the ambulance; Washington and Harry followed in the car. At the hospital Dr. Hondo disappeared with the patients behind the forbidding "No Admittance" sign. Ohara and Washington were left to wait outside.

They bought coffee from a machine and sat down on a bench just outside the operating rooms. Ohara sipped the strong black brew with little enthusiasm. It was something to do while they waited for news. But Washington wanted some answers. "Sam," he said, "have you read the confession yet? What gives?"

Ohara set down his paper cup on a nearby table and took the still unopened envelope out of his pocket. He unsealed it and pulled out several folded sheets. When he spread them out, Washington stared at the long rows of Japanese characters. "Can you read that?"

In reply Ohara began to translate.

Ohara-san, I am sorry for the trouble I cause. Please forgive me. Now I want you to understand all.

I knew that if the police found out what happened they would take my Yumi and shut her up in prison for crazy ones. She would die there, frightened and alone, away from everyone she knows I cannot let that happen.

Ohara's voice roughened on the last words and he paused a moment before going on.

I want you to understand also about Kenji, because it is for his sake too that I must do this terrible thing. Since his parents died, he has been my son. He grew up with Yumi. Even as a little boy he loved her, played with her and took care of her always. He brought his good friend, Miguel, to be Yumi's friend, too. The boys treated her like a small princess. They played they were her samurai. Children are strange, are they not?

There was a look on Ohara's face Washington wished he could fathom. He was tempted to ask a question, but Ohara had begun to read again.

Even now, Kenji is trying to protect Yumi. He did not tell you the truth, but I will.

That night, because I had an appointment at home, I left the store early. When I did not at first see Yumi, I went to the workshop. When I opened the door, I could not believe what was there. Everything— shelves, dolls, cases were thrown down. My Yumi was standing by the table staring at the floor, holding her gold *kanzashi* in her hand. Her dress was torn and her hair was fallen down on her shoulders. Most terrible, on her dress and hands there was blood.

I ran to her and almost fell over a man on the floor. Blood was coming from his throat. He did not move or breathe. It was the man who had bought Yumi's doll, and he was dead. Then I saw Kenji on the floor.

[146]

I was afraid he was dead, too, and went to him to see. But praise Buddha, he was not; he was unconscious, but still breathing.

Yumi began to cry and shake, so I must leave Kenji and go to her. She did not know me, but I got her to the house and gave her medicine to make her sleep. Then I went back to Kenji.

His eyes were open but he was in much pain. He told me he had found the man choking Yumi, tearing her clothes. Kenji tried to pull him away, but the man was a strong fighter. Soon Kenji was beaten and knocked down. He didn't remember anything more.

But I knew. I had seen Yumi holding the *kanzashi*. I had seen the blood on her hands and clothes. She had killed the man. I had to tell Kenji. We were both afraid for Yumi, so we made a plan. I cleaned everything. Late at night he helped me put the man's body in our car and I took him away. I found a place with lots of bushes and put him there.

Washington shook his head, visualizing that small, tough old woman getting rid of Morgan's body. "How did she ever do it? The weight must have half killed her."

"When you're as desperate as she was, you find the strength," Ohara said. He went back to the letter.

At first we thought it would be all right, but it was not.

Now I have told you everything that happened. In a little while I will put my Yumi to sleep. I have a good medicine—no pain, no frightening. Then I will make amends for the terrible thing I have done. I will die in the honorable way of our ancestors. You understand, Ohara-san, there will be no shame, no one will despise.

Please tell my son, Kenji, that I am very proud of

him. He must sell the store so he can learn to be a good doctor. Make him see that he must not be sad. Yumi and I are safe. I thank you.

Hana Kubota

"No one will despise, Hana," Ohara said as he folded up the letter and replaced it in the envelope. Then he stood up and walked over to the window of the lounge. His face was hidden, but Washington saw his tightly clenched fists and the defeated slope of his broad, straight shoulders. There was nothing Washington could think of to say. Ohara was paying the price of allowing himself to become personally involved. In his own way Washington had done the same; the crushed paper cup he was mashing between his fingers was evidence of that. He dropped it into a wastebasket and stared down at the green tiled floor.

Neither man seemed to want to talk; caught up in their own thoughts, they were unaware how much time had passed until a sibilant swoosh of sound turned both their heads at once toward the swinging green doors that led to the operating rooms.

Dr. Hondo was walking toward them. "The girl will be all right, Sam. It was a good thing you found the empty vial. I was able to identify the medicine, old as Japan almost, but simple to make up. We pumped her out, gave an antidote and a sedative." He smiled a little as he watched Ohara's reaction. "One thing, though, when she wakes up there should be someone she recognizes with her. Otherwise the psychological trauma could be devastating."

"We can get Kenji," Ohara said. "How long do we have?"

"I'd say you have about three hours before she wakes up."

"What about Hana Kubota?" Washington's question was professional, his expression was not.

"We've done what we can, but she's barely conscious and is doing her best to die."

"I'd like to see her," Ohara said.

"It won't help, Sam. She can't talk. No way you can get a statement."

"I know, but it's important that I see her."

Dr. Hondo studied Ohara. "No matter what she did, she's a damn brave woman. Come on."

Minutes later Ohara and Dr. Hondo stood looking down on Hana Kubota's small square figure encased in the white womb of the hospital bed. She lay unmoving, her eyes closed. To Washington standing behind them, it seemed she was almost gone.

Ohara touched one of the folded hands that lay on top of the sheet. It was cold. He put it between his own hands, trying to impart some of the life-giving energy of their warmth. As the hand in his grasp moved he said softly in Japanese, "Hana-san, it's Ohara. I have your letter. I understand."

She seemed to stop even the shallow breath that sustained her life, then slowly opened her eyes and looked at him. Tears welled up and spilled over onto her cheeks. She tried to speak, but no sound came. The word her lips formed was "Yumi."

"Yumi's going to be all right; she's in the hospital, too. Dr. Hondo here is my good friend; he will protect Yumi and take good care of her. You don't need to worry."

A brightness lit her face only to fade as rational thought followed. She closed her eyes, her lips pressed tight.

"Hana." Ohara's voice was insistent. "You must open your eyes and look at me. I have something important to tell you." He waited, letting the silence draw out until at last she opened her eyes. "Listen to me, Hana. Yumi did not kill the man. The police will not take her away."

Hana made a slight negative movement with her head. "Hana, listen. Yumi got the blood on her hands and dress because she touched the man after he was killed. That's all."

[149]

Incredulity, then joy shone in Hana's eyes for a moment, then a new terror struck her. Her fingers clawed as she tried to pull Ohara closer and forced words past her mangled throat. "Not…Kenji…"

"No, we know now who killed the man—not Kenji, not Yumi, not you. You are safe, everything will be all right."

Her eyes opened fully to search his, to be sure it was truth he spoke. With a feeble gesture she tried to draw Ohara's hands to her lips but the effort was too much. Sighing, she seemed to relax into sleep and her fingers fell away from his. Dr. Hondo moved Ohara aside and bent over her. "She's gone," he said.

"Did I do it?" Ohara was visibly shaken.

"No, it was inevitable."

"I only wanted her to know it was all right—keep her from being afraid anymore."

"I think you did," Dr. Hondo said. "Look at her."

Hana's square plain face looked peaceful, almost beautiful. Ohara could not regret what he had done.

Washington said nothing until they once again were in the waiting room. He touched Ohara on the arm. "What did you tell her?"

"Ted, I'm sorry about the Japanese. I told her we knew neither Yumi nor Kenji had killed the man, nor had she. That everything would be all right."

"I guess it made it easier for her at the end. You did the right thing."

"I told her the absolute truth."

"Come on, she confessed that Yumi had blood on her hands and clothes. She was holding the dagger."

"True, but I think Yumi touched Morgan after he was killed; she was holding the *kanzashi* to defend herself."

"I know how you feel, but it's still guesswork."

"That part, yes, but I told Hana something else. I told her we now knew who had killed Morgan."

"And how long have *we* known?" Washington asked after a moment's silence.

"I got the glimmer of an idea this morning and I've been fitting pieces in all day. I haven't seen you to tell you, but it's solid."

"I'm here now, Sam. Give me a name."

"A boy named Miguel. Come on, I'll tell you about it while we try to get Kenji out of jail. We don't have much time."

XXII

ARRANGING for Kenji's release was no simple matter. It helped that Judge Robert Tanaka was available, and sympathetic when he heard the circumstances.

It was even more difficult telling Kenji what had happened. He was stunned and bitter, and the news that he'd been cleared meant little to him. "I gave you what you wanted," he shouted. "Why didn't you let it alone?"

"Because it wasn't the truth," Ohara shot back. "You didn't kill Morgan."

"Oh, my God! Why did she do it?" Kenji covered his face with his hands. "She knew I would save Yumi."

"She did it because she didn't want you to sacrifice yourself for them. She wrote that in a letter to me."

"What will happen to Yumi now?" Kenji's voice was a defeated whisper.

"She'll get expert care from a doctor friend of mine who thinks she may not be retarded and may even be able to speak."

Kenji stared at him, dumbfounded. "Yumi might talk and be well?"

Ohara watched happiness flood Kenji's face and felt a lump in his own throat. "Right now, the doctor wants someone she knows with her, so we'll get you over there as fast as we can. Now sit down while we finish up the formalities."

Taking the dazed boy by the arm, Ohara sat him down. Then he took Hana's letter out of his pocket and put it in Kenji's hands. "I want you to read this so that when you think about Hana Kubota you will remember only how much she

[153]

loved both her children. Respect her courage, and justify her faith in you."

Everything was at last in order. Ohara came to take Kenji to the patrol car that would get him to the hospital quickly, but first Kenji handed back the letter and grasped Ohara's hand. "Thank you for letting me read it; I understand now. And thanks for everything else."

Watching the car drive off, Washington felt good. "This job has its rewards sometimes, doesn't it? You pulled more strings than a politician to send him back to Yumi."

"Yes." Ohara grinned. "Sometimes you need a few short-cuts."

"Well, what now? Time to collect Morgan's killer?"

"Yes," Ohara agreed. "Let me get my briefcase and we'll go see him."

A short time later they were sitting in one of the interrogation rooms in the county jail waiting to interview a prisoner. The briefcase lay open on the table as Ohara once more studied the inmate's file. He did not look up when the door opened and a man was ushered in. Washington, watching the prisoner's face, saw his casual curiosity change to uneasiness.

Ohara continued to absorb himself in the file and Washington followed his lead. The waiting police secretary looked down at his notebook as the silence grew. The prisoner shifted his feet restlessly and clasped his arms across his thin body, which looked too small for the regulation prison blue denims. He glanced apprehensively around, then almost unwillingly moved toward the table. "You guys want to see me?" His voice was unsteady and he cleared his throat noisily to hide it.

Ohara looked up. "Yes, Miguel. Sit down."

Surprise flashed across the prisoner's narrow face as he

obeyed. "What you call me that for?" A nervous grin stretched his mouth.

"It says here that's your name—Miguel Yzaguirre, AKA Flaco." Ohara's eyes were intent. "Is it or isn't it?"

"Yeah, sure, that's my name. But only my mama calls me Miguel anymore."

"We ran across someone else who called you Miguel." Washington's deep voice drew an apprehensive glance.

"Who?"

"We'll get to that later," Ohara said evenly, "but first I have a few questions. Do you want a lawyer present?"

Flaco shook his head in disgust. "What for? All that meathead ever tells me is 'cop a plea.' Some lawyer!"

"Very well." Ohara reached into the attache case and took out a knife. The harsh overhead light flashed along its needle blade and highlighted the rich gold design of the handle. It was a beautiful piece of weaponry except for the small jagged hook at the tip. The police property tag was still tied to the handle. Flaco reached out his left hand to pick it up, but Ohara held it firmly on the table.

"Is this your knife?"

"Sure that's mine. Ain't nobody else got a knife with a crest like that." Flaco's pride was obvious. "It's a first-class shiv."

Ohara picked up a piece of paper, plunged the knife through, then withdrew it. The hole it made was symmetrical except for a small scarring break on the side. "Too bad about the tip." He studied the hole in the paper.

"Works good though, and take a look at that crest."

Washington picked up the knife and looked it over. "It's different all right. What's the writing say?" He pointed to the raised lettering on the hilt. "Is it Spanish?"

"*Muerte.*" Flaco grinned. "That means death. Good, huh?"

From a manila envelope full of pictures, Ohara extracted

[155]

one and held it out to Flaco. It was an enlargement of a man's extended arm, blown up enough to show clearly a puncture wound with the same jagged tear as the hole in the paper. Just above the wound an old scar angled around the biceps. "Think your knife could have done that?"

Flaco started to take the picture, then abruptly withdrew his hand. "How should I know, man? I never seen nothin' like that before."

"I've seen it before." Ohara held out a second picture. "It's on my arm."

Flaco stared at the second picture of Ohara stripped to the waist, his arm extended, the wound with the scar above it plainly visible.

"So what?"

Silently Ohara laid out a third picture, an enlargement of a man's throat with a puncture at the base. The wound was perfectly round with no jagged tear at the base. Flaco flicked the picture with a finger. "Muerte didn' do that one. Who's the guy?"

"Name's Lopez," Ohara said offhandedly. "A Nuestra Familia hit man got him."

"What's the point?" Flaco's words came out tight and pinched, the usual arrogance missing.

Ohara laid down a fourth enlargement beside the Lopez picture, again a man's throat with a puncture wound. This wound had a small ragged tear on one side, similar to the hole he had made in the paper with Flaco's knife and to the photograph of the wound on Ohara's arm. "Muerte made this one," he said. "That's Morgan."

Flaco sat very still, panic showing in his eyes and the quick flaring breath in his nostrils. Then his street instincts took over. "You guys are crazy. So I stuck you, but I got an alibi for when Morgan was killed, my lawyer says so. That picture's a fake."

[156]

"It's not a fake," Ohara said. "It's a duplicate." He pulled out the official autopsy file on Morgan with detailed pictures of the body. An eight by ten of the one he'd shown Flaco was among them.

"I don' give a shit for pictures, man. I was with Chino when Morgan was killed. You find him; he'll tell you."

"We did find him. He says he was pulling a job in the Valley around five. Then he had to fence it. He didn't get home until midnight. Then you were at his place waiting for him."

Flaco wet his lips. "Well, maybe I didn' remember the times so good. I wasn' with him on the job, but I was at his place all the time and you can't prove no different."

Washington shook his head. "Wrong, Flaco. Burglary picked up Chino's old lady for receiving. She claims she was waiting for him in his apartment and she didn't mention you or anybody else."

Flaco seemed to draw into himself. "I'm not talkin' no more. I want my lawyer."

Ohara nodded and began putting the pictures back into the briefcase. Flaco stood up. "Let me out of here." He turned toward the door.

"By the way," Ohara said, "we have a witness who can probably place you in the vicinity at the time Morgan was killed."

"More bull!" Flaco sneered. "Who would that be?"

"A librarian, who can very likely identify you from a picture as the man shaking down Morgan's car in the library parking lot."

"What are you smokin', man? Morgan wasn' killed in no parkin' lot; they did him in the bushes. Maybe he was takin' a leak."

"No, he wasn't killed in the bushes where he was found. He was killed at the Kubota house, in Yumi's workshop a block away from where you were seen."

"So maybe I looked at his car. No crime lookin'."

"We have another witness who saw you."

"Nobody coulda saw me—" Flaco blurted out, then stopped.

"How can you be sure?" Washington asked mildly.

"Fuck you, I don' have to answer nothin'."

"Incidentally," Ohara said, "your friend Kenji told us what happened to Yumi."

There was a long moment when Flaco's eyes grew blank, then he sat down in the chair as if his legs would no longer hold him. "You tryin' to tell me Kenji fingered me?"

"He didn't finger you," Washington said. "He showed us how he killed Morgan."

"Kenji kill Morgan? Man, he was always playin' samurai, but he couldn' fight his way out of a paper bag."

"We know he didn't kill Morgan," Ohara agreed. "He was trying to protect someone. Morgan beat him unconscious for one thing; for another, he's not left-handed."

As if jerked by strings Flaco pulled both his hands into his lap.

"There's another more likely suspect," Ohara went on, seeming not to notice.

"Who?" Flaco's eyes lifted to Ohara and seemed to hang there.

"Yumi Kubota."

"You're out of your skull. Yumi was—Yumi wouldn' kill anybody."

"We didn't think so, but her mother wrote a confession."

Flaco's face drained of color as he jerked to the edge of his chair. "What could she confess?"

"That she came home, found Morgan dead on the floor and Yumi standing over him holding a dagger, with blood on her hands and clothes. She was afraid the police would take Yumi away and lock her up so she tried to protect her in the best way she could. She gave her a lethal dose of sleeping medicine, then stabbed herself."

"Oh, God." The barely heard words were full of pain. "Is she—"

"No, we got them to the hospital. Yumi will be all right, but Mrs. Kubota is dead."

"She should be after doin' that to Yumi."

"She was only trying to protect her—the way you and Kenji used to protect her. She mentioned Yumi's two samurai in her letter, Kenji and Miguel."

Flaco was silent a long time, then said, "So that's how you got it—the Miguel. That was a long time ago." He sat silent, thinking, then said, "What will happen to Yumi now?"

"That's up to the courts. The confession is pretty heavy."

"She'll be OK. They won' hold her, after what happened."

"Maybe not in jail, but under the circumstances she could be committed to a mental hospital."

"God, man, you gotta do somethin'."

"I'll present my case against you"—Ohara nodded to the pictures—"along with my evidence, but the confession letter will go in the record with her mother's eyewitness account. It's fifty-fifty either way."

"What you're sayin', man, you ain't sure you can keep Yumi out of the crazy farm?"

Ohara nodded.

Flaco leaned back. He looked drained, but his lips moved slightly into what might have been a smile. "I always was a sucker for that samurai bit. Kenji and me, we wouldn' let nobody look cross-eyed at Yumi. We took on some tough dudes."

"Just like you took on Morgan." Washington's voice was almost friendly.

Flaco didn't hear him; he was thinking of something else.

[159]

"You know I didn' mind gettin' beat up those days. Yumi always stroked my face so nice and looked so sad. I wish my mama and me had never moved away. Later on, I couldn' go back." He straightened then and looked over at the secretary. "Tell that guy to write this down and get it straight."

The officer sat forward, waiting, his pencil lifted. Flaco nodded, satisfied.

"Morgan was always shitty to me. I hated his guts. I hated the way he looked at Yumi and I warned him to stay away. When I saw him at the carnival with that hard type, I figured maybe I was on to somethin'. I followed him that night, and a lot after that. I was on his tail the day he parked at the library. I thought maybe I should check the car. That's a good place to hide a stash. Then that old dame saw me and banged on the window. I got outta there and was goin' down the alley by Yumi's yard. I figured I'd duck in and say hello for old time's sake."

Flaco stopped and ran his hand through his stringy hair. "Gotta cigarette?"

Washington lit one and handed it to him. Flaco's hands shook as he took it. "Anyway, Morgan was there, just followin' Yumi into the workshop. It worried me. She's just a little kid—a guy like Morgan could take her before she knew what was happenin'. I waited a few minutes to see if they'd come out. I was just goin' over to see what was happenin' when Kenji comes outta the house. He goes in the garage and pretty soon I hear the fight. I hadda go in then. When I opened the door, Yumi was layin' on the floor like she was dead and Morgan had Kenji down and was gettin' ready to chop him. He was laughin', enjoyin' himself. The bastard never heard me comin'. I pulled his goddamn head back and slid the shiv right in."

Flaco drew on the cigarette and shrugged. "That's what happened."

The room was quiet after the fast spate of words. Flaco watched as the secretary finished writing. "Yumi'll be all right now, won't she, none of them mental places?"

"She'll be all right," Ohara said.

"I mean you guys'll leave her and Kenji alone now?"

"We have your confession, don't we?" Washington answered.

"Yeah, my confession." A ghost of a grin touched Flaco's face. "And you can prove it, too...all them pictures."

"Yes, Miguel," Ohara said, "we can prove it."

"You're pretty smart, you know? Well, I guess that's that then." Flaco looked somehow at a loss, as if there should be something more at a time like this. "You want me to sign somethin'?" Now that his moment of decision was over, he'd become again only a thin-faced Chicano in oversized jail clothes.

"You can sign the statement when it's typed." Ohara stood up, looking very tall, very Japanese. There was no satisfaction in winning this one.

"Hey, would you do me a favor?"

"If I can."

"Tell Kenji Miguel says take care of Yumi."

"I'll do that."

Flaco got up. "And get me some word about her sometime. You do that, man!" Then he walked over to the door and knocked to be let out.

When he had gone, Ohara picked up the small flawed dagger and held it a moment before he put it back into the briefcase. It was too small for a samurai sword, but nevertheless, that's what it had become.

Washington and Ohara were silent as they left the gray bulk of the county jail and walked toward the parking lot. When they reached the car, Washington said, "I'll drive."

As they pulled out, Washington looked over at him. "Funny thing, I thought I'd be pretty bucked up at nailing that little punk, but I'm not."

Ohara sighed. "I know. It should have been Morgan we nailed." He leaned back and closed his eyes. As they drove, the kaleidoscope of the case revolved in his mind, full of faces he couldn't forget...Hana, Flaco, Kenji, Morgan's father and, above all, Yumi. For the first time he admitted to himself why he'd cared so much. It was Yumi's face he'd remember longest.

Washington drove in silence for a while, then tuned in the radio news, keeping the volume low. A familiar name caught his attention, Ohara heard it too. "Leo Krepp, crusading reporter, is recovering in the hospital from a vicious mugging. He says he is unable to describe his assailants..."

Washington shook his head in disgust. "Unsure my foot—shit scared is more like it. Too bad he wasn't crusading enough to put his money where his mouth is."

"Looks like Lucky Montero got lucky again," Ohara commented.

The news report was continuing. "Krepp says he will continue to be the public's watchdog and turn the spotlight on the fire department in his next series."

"God help them," Washington said as he snapped off the radio. "Well, with Krepp bugging the fire department maybe we'll be able to cool the gang fracas, now that they've got their eye for an eye."

"I hope you're right." Ohara didn't sound optimistic.

"Oh, by the way, Sam, mind if I stop and make a pickup on the way?"

"No." Ohara settled back and in a few minutes they were slowing to a stop in a small shopping center not far from the station—a deli, a vet's, a cleaner's, a supermarket. Washington got out of the car. "Won't be a minute."

In a short time Ohara heard the back door of the car open. A large shaggy mutt on a brand new leash leaped into the backseat and spread his rangy bulk across it. He looked considerably cleaner than when Ohara had last seen him.

"Isn't that our material witness?" he asked.

"That's him." Washington grinned. "I bailed him out of the pound and got him cleaned up. I can guarantee his appearance in court if you need him."

Ohara laughed, feeling good. "What are you going to call him?" Two oversize paws clamped on Washington's shoulders as he slid behind the steering wheel. Ohara scratched the shaggy brown ears.

"Well, I'll tell you." Washington took his time, concentrating on the traffic. "I figure he's got a way with him, and he sort of grows on you, too. I've decided to call him Irish—if you don't mind, Ohara."